WE RUN NEW YORK
A GHETTO GAME OF THRONES

SA'ID SALAAM

URBAN AESOP PUBLICATIONS

Copyright © 2022 by Sa'id Salaam

All rights reserved.

No part of this book may be reproduced in any form or by any electronic or mechanical means, including information storage and retrieval systems, without written permission from the author, except for the use of brief quotations in a book review.

Email: saidmsalaam@gmail.com

Cover: Adriane Hall

Proofreader: KaiCee White

"Love whom you love mildly, perhaps he will become hateful to you someday. Hate whom you hate mildly, perhaps he will become your beloved someday." The Prophet Muhammad peace and blessings be upon him.

CHAPTER 1

1993 HARLEM, NY

"Ooh that's way too much ass for them Jordache mami!" Rosalinda squealed as Jennifer turned sideways to admire her ass in the mirror. She had a penchant for being dramatic when it came to complimenting the boss's daughter but this wasn't that. That really was a lot of ass rounding out those jeans.

"Nah, chica," she said and turned to the other side. She cupped her full breast and let them drop, before puckering her glossy lips. "That's just the right amount of ass!"

"For real tho, them black girls ain't got shit on us boricuas!" Rosalinda shot back with a mix of pride and racism.

The devil did his job and most of mankind declared its superiority over the rest of mankind just off their race or ethnicity. Which was weird since Puerto Ricans ran the gamut of hues and textures. Like God made a people stew mixed with various shades and textures.

Jennifer's own mother was as white as any Caucasian, while her dad had a medium brown complexion and could pass for a black man until he opened his mouth. Still he took more pride in his tiny ancestral island than his new home in New York city. Which was weird too since Puerto Rico is part of America anyway.

Devilish as it may have been, Miguel Camacho's superiority complex propelled him to the top of the food chain in Spanish Harlem. Not an easy feat in an area filled with Columbians, Cubans and Dominicans all vying for the top spot.

He believed that most of life's problems can be solved by throwing money at it. Miguel chunked duffle bags full of cash to the Columbians and became their number one distributor. Now, the Cubans, Dominicans and blacks had to buy from him or go uptown to the Bronx or head out to Brooklyn. Both were extremely dangerous so they shopped with him. He found that the rest of life's problems can be solved with violence. Miguel had no problem with extreme acts of violence that left a lasting impression on friends and foes alike.

Miguel hoped for a son each time his darling wife Esmeralda got pregnant. Most didn't make it full term until Jennifer came along. He hoped for a prince but had to settle for his princess. The now seventeen year old was by far the prettiest in her hood, if not borough.

Jennifer ended up half a hue lighter than her father and inherited the ass his mother's mother inherited from her ancestors in Africa. The heavy breasts were all from Esmeralda's side of the family. The delicate facial features were a mix of both parents. His thick lips, her thin nose, her round chin, his cheek bones. While she adopted her physical traits through genetics the attitude was all her own.

Being the boss's daughter meant she heard him boss a lot

of people most of her life. Including her mother who in turn bossed all of her subordinates. As a result Esmeralda became bossy and told her daughter most of what to do and say. Even who to date since the only dates her overprotective papi permitted was today's date on the calendar. That's why he had a fit when she stepped out of her room to head out for the night.

"No!" Miguel announced in a one word protest when his daughter came out from her room. The tight T-shirt showed more than he wanted to see so it was a good thing he turned his head before seeing all that ass.

"Tranquilo papi," his wife purred and let her hand slip into his crotch. He may have ruled his hood by force but she ruled him with sex. Even the promise of sex was enough to get her way most times. This time too since he grumbled to himself and let it go. "Ju look nice mami. Where ju guys going?"

"Just skating," Jennifer lied and kissed her cheek. The skating rink was just uptown so it was close enough for comfort.

"Have fun," Esmeralda said and pressed a roll of cash into her hand. The woman firmly believed a fat wad of cash was an accessory every woman should carry.

"Thank you mami," she gushed and headed out the door. She had to tuck the cash into her bra since her pants were too tight to use her pockets.

"Follow them Pipo," Miguel ordered as soon as his daughter cleared the apartment.

"On it!" the newest member of his security staff barked and headed out behind him. He was recently promoted after putting in some work on a Dominican crew who set up shop on a block that wasn't theirs to set up shop on. The Camacho funeral home gave them a nice send off.

Jennifer felt like a celebrity when she stepped out onto the block her father ran. Time stopped for a moment while the locals jocked her. The fellas bit their bottom lips at what they would do with that fat ass, while the chicks just admired her Jordache jeans, tight T and bright Reeboks.

"I love summer in New York!" Jennifer cheered as the top came down on her BMW 325.

"Me too!" Rosalinda agreed since she too did love summer in New York. Plus she was a sidekick and that was her job. She cosigned, agreed, enabled and facilitated her every whim. Well, most of them since everyone has their own agenda. "Where are we going?"

"Ju will see," Jennifer laughed as she drove past the block that would have taken them to the rink. She turned the knob on the radio so people could sing Ladi dadi along with Slick Rick and Dougie Fresh, booming through her system.

"Where are they going?" Pipo pondered when they missed the turn they should have made. A group of young chicks caught his eye as he drove by so he pulled over to flirt. He would catch up at the rink and stay on her heels all night. Except Jennifer had other plans that didn't include rolling around in circles.

"Where are we going?" Rosalinda asked again when she pulled onto the hundred and fifty ninth street bridge. On one side was Manhattan but the other was another land known as the Boogie down Bronx.

"To see Wutang at the Fever!" she cheered and wiggled her ass in the seat.

"Es muy peligroso!" her friend warned, and she was correct. The Bronx was a very dangerous part of a very dangerous city. In truth it was no worse than the hood they just came from. But the danger you know is less dangerous than the danger you don't know.

"My father is Miguel Camacho! I go wherever I want!" Jennifer huffed indignantly at the notion. Like many kids from rich and powerful people she held an air of privilege.

She was partially right though because her father's name rang not just bells but church bells. His organization dropped so many bodies he bought a funeral home. Ironically some of his victims' families paid the debts that got them stretched out through funeral costs. One time one family didn't pay so he had their loved one dumped in front of their building.

"Ju right chica," Rosalinda nodded, but still hit the lock on the locked door to make sure it was locked. As futile as it may have been since the top was dropped. A few turns later they were headed towards the iconic Disco Fever.

"We need some weed!" Jennifer decided and scanned the nearby park for a dealer. Her father's organization sold coke, weed, smack and crack but no one dared sell her a weed seed, let alone a whole bag. Luckily the park near the club contained several dealers, dealing for their daily bread.

"Trey bags! Got that Buddha bless!" a handsome young dealer called Buddha called out to the passersby in the darkened park. His charismatic smile, smooth dark brown skin and incongruent hazel eyes got him sales from women and girls who didn't even smoke weed. Once he put some weight on his wiry six foot two inch frame he could be a male model. Not that he would be since he was content with being a pretty thug.

He was from the self contained world right up the steps on 167th street made famous to the world in The Joker movie years later but they were always famous in the Bronx. His Highbridge neighborhood did brisk business for his small-time weed operation but the heavy traffic going to the club was good money on a Saturday night.

"Nah yo! We selling these shits as nicks!" Buddha's partnership Rip reminded. His real name was Gabriel Sanchez but his dark skin and coarse hair made him look more like a Leroy Johnson. The two had been friends since kindergarten and shared the struggle of growing up fatherless in the ghetto. Being fatherless anywhere would be rough, Highbridge made it rougher. As a result these two eighteen year olds were as rough as the concrete jungle that raised them.

"Nicks! Get yo nicks right here!" Buddha switched just as a group of fly girls stomped through on the way to the club. "Sup ladies. Y'all smoking or nah?"

"We good," one shot back with a mouthful of B-girl venom. Only because she kept her eyes straight ahead and hand on her straight razor in her purse. Her friend not only looked but liked what she saw.

"Hole up ma. Let me see what shorty working with," she told her friend and looked Buddha over.

"Nicks of that Buddha bless!" he reiterated and held out a couple of bags in his palm. Weed was sold in tiny manila envelopes back then so she had to open one to check out the quality.

"Them shits is trey bags on Third ave!" the first girl huffed as her friend opened the bag.

"Buddha?" she dared once she inhaled the product. She

twisted her lips at the brand he put on the regular, brownish weed.

"Tye stick?" Buddha offered along with that smile that was going to get him a lot of pussy in life.

"How bout some regular ass weed!" she shot back and twisted her lips. Lots of people were selling the more exotic chocolate, Lambs bread, Tye stick and Buddha but all these fledgling dealers could get at the moment was regular weed from the Jamaicans downtown. It would still get you high and that's all that matters.

"And they treys!" her friend added. Nonetheless, the girl fished a twenty from her purse and pressed it into his palm. She plucked four of the three dollar bags from his hand and walked off.

"Son, ma was jocking!" Rip announced as they both watched the wiggling assess wiggle away towards the club.

"Word!" Buddha agreed. Movement from the side stole his attention from the booty show. A well known stick up kid from University projects was creeping through the darkness. Buddha shifted a little just so he could feel the Saturday night special tucked into his waistband. He felt no fear in general but especially since they grew up together in Highbridge.

"Here come Black Rob," Rip whispered when he picked him up a few seconds later. A few seconds late can easily be a few seconds too late in the streets.

"Sup Black?" Buddha asked since they weren't cool enough to just kick it. If it wasn't business he could kick rocks as far as he was concerned.

"Let me get a trey?" he asked and tilted his head like people do when they try you up.

"Let me get three bucks!" Rip shot back. He had a twenty

two automatic in his pocket but neither had bust nothing. Yet that is because it was inevitable in this line of work.

"I got y'all after I catch a lick," he said since he was in the darkened park for business as well. The dark and dangerous park saw enough traffic to catch a few licks before heading up the hill to Highbridge.

"Fuck..." Rip began but Buddha cut in before he reached the 'outa here'.

"Word," he said and happily passed off the trey bag. The two friends were equals but Rip accepted the fact that his friend was somewhat smarter than him. After all, Buddha did just graduate from high school and he never would. Not that he couldn't, he just wasn't interested. He was cool being a hood nigga and you certainly don't need a diploma for that.

"What you do that for?" Rip asked once Black melted back into the darkness like a lion in tall grass. "That nigga ain't never gonna pay up!"

"Son, we just bought a whole nigga for three bucks! Now he can't never ask for shit again," Buddha explained. It made perfect sense but sometimes sense didn't make sense to Rip.

"Fuck that, I want my three bucks!" he grumbled. Three dollars was a lot and could do a lot in those days. Especially for poor kids of poor parents with poor parenting skills. Despite welfare and food stamps they often had to get it from the mud.

Three dollars done right could get a turkey and cheese hero, quart carton of juice, chips, chocolate chip cookies and a loose Newport in any bodega. Some would throw in a free White Owl cigar to roll up the next blunt.

"Word," his friend replied. Not that he agreed, it's just easier sometimes to just say word and be done with it.

"Ok then! Two bad bitches in the rag top Beemer!" Rip

announced when the sporty sports car pulled to a stop. The top raised before they stepped out. Both watched as the two hotties stepped from the car and looked around. They weren't the only cheeba dealers out so the girls had their choice. They looked over Buddha and Rip, then overlooked them in favor of a group of Latino dealers playing salsa music from a boombox.

"Hola mamacita!" one called out as the girls made their way over.

Their bright, gold jewelry seemed to light up the night and that's not good. Once again it was Buddha who spotted the danger a few seconds before his partner. Black Rob eased forward with a black gun at his side. He fell in step so he could kill a few birds with whatever bullets his revolver held. Meaning rob the girls and the dealers at the same time.

"Oh shit..." Rip proclaimed when he finally caught on his customary few seconds later. Both knew what was going to happen and had no choice but to let it happen.

The Bronx was affectionately known as the Boogie down but a lesser known moniker is 'mind your business'. Stick ups were Black Rob's business so they would mind theirs and sell their weed. The robber popped out just as the girls reached the Puerto Rican dealer's bench. He decided to rob the guys and girls at the same time.

"Run all dat!" Black Rob announced with a sinister chuckle. He was going to spend their cash, smoke their weed and rock their jewels. All that and still not pay Buddha for the trey bag.

"Oh shit!" Buddha laughed when the dealers did the unexpected. They hopped down off the bench and took off running in different directions.

"Wow!" Rip laughed but wouldn't laugh long. One girl began to remove her jewelry but the other put up a protest.

"I am Jennifer Camacho! Miguel Camacho's daughter! I'm not giving you shit!" Jennifer protested and took a swing at him with her Gucci bag. Buddha cracked a smile since she had heart but Black Rob cracked her jaw.

"Oh shit!" he exclaimed when the robber dropped the girl with a right hook. He spun and knocked the other one down as well.

"Come off all this shit!" he growled and began snatching the chains from their necks. Rosalinda put up no resistance but Jennifer was cut from the same rugged cloth as her father. She put up a fight for hers until Black Rob socked her again in her eye.

"Ju got that," Jennifer nodded. One eye was closed but she mentally took pictures of the man with the other so she could describe him in vivid detail to her father. Black Rob took it a step further and fondled her breast. He looked around and made a life changing decision.

"Take them pants off!" he demanded. He could definitely sell the expensive jeans but was after something far more valuable. He had no idea the girl was a virgin but planned to rape her anyway. "Bout to fuck the shit out yo fine ass bitch!"

"Fuck you going?" Rip asked when Buddha took off in their direction. There was no time to explain to him so Buddha just explained to the would-be rapist.

"Yo son, you bugging!" he announced when he reached the robber. Jennifer focused her one eye on him to take his picture too. He was dying too just for being out here. She would have the attendant at the gas station murdered too for not washing her windows. The Camacho funeral home was about to get real busy over tonight's happenings. Some people are just not to be fucked with. Jennifer Camacho was one of those people.

"Say what?" Black Rob asked with his face straining to understand why he was in his business. Even Rip couldn't figure it out and they were best friends for life.

"Bruh, you got their bread and jewels. Take the money and run," he suggested while the man still struggled to get her pants off.

"Tell you what..." Black Rob growled and began to turn his gun in that direction. He was a known shooter so Buddha didn't wait to get shot. He whipped out his own gun before he saw the black hole that could put a hole in him. Flight or fight kicked in and his body went into autopilot. He watched as the gun bucked and sent a slug right into Black Rob's right eye.

"Yooooo!" Rip shouted when the same slug came out the back of his head. He may have been stuck but Buddha remained calm.

"Y'all get up! Get out of here!" he told the fallen girls. He reached for Jennifer's hand to help her up but she initially pulled away.

The girl was so shaken by nearly being raped. She looked over and the mangled mess that was once a stick up kid and snapped out of it. She accepted the helping hand and climbed to her feet. Rosalinda was on her own since Rip wasn't as chivalrous as his friend.

"Puto!" Jennifer growled and kicked Black Rob in his head. She slipped in the puddle of blood and went back down.

"We must be waiting for five-o?" Rip wondered since they were still at a murder scene. It was a justifiable homicide but they weren't planning on waiting around for the cops to come.

"Let's bounce!" Buddha agreed and turned to leave once he helped Jennifer back to her feet.

"Don't leave us! I can't fucking see!" Jennifer shouted since her eye was completely swollen shut from the blow. More like demanded like a diva, used to demanding people.

"Have your girl push the whip!" Rip shouted since he was ready to run up those tall ass stairs and go home.

"I can't drive!" Rosalinda moaned. Like quite a few New Yorkers spoiled off trains, buses, ferries, taxis and gypsy cabs, never would learn to drive.

"Fuck!" Buddha shouted and conceded. He took the outstretched keys and pulled Jennifer along to her car. A few minutes later they crossed back over to Manhattan. A few minutes later they reached their block. That's when all hell broke out.

CHAPTER 2

"Oye!" a worker announced to get attention. That's what they say to take note, or look-it when something or someone needed attention. Had it been police cries of mahando, or Five-O would resonate up and down Fifth avenue. This time he spotted Jennifer's BMW on Fifth ave. It wasn't hard to spot since it was the only cherry red convertible in the city. The call would carry all the way up the block through the series of corner boys and lookouts employed by the Camacho organization.

"What the fuck?" one of the watchers needed to know when he saw the two black men in the front seat of the bosses car. He took off after it on foot repeating the call, "Oye!"

"Uh-oh..." Rip murmured when he saw all the attention. More boys, teens and grown men joined the chase up Fifth avenue. Most didn't even know what was going on but the mean mugs were contagious and everyone looked angry.

"Don't worry about them," Jennifer assured since she

knew most of the angry faces following behind. "Turn on One nineteenth."

"Here?" Buddha asked rhetorically since he was turning. The crowd was half a block behind but the calls of 'Oye' reached the block when they turned onto it.

"A-yo, you sure we good?" Buddha asked behind him but Jennifer didn't get the chance to answer before the car doors were snatched open. Both he and Rip were snatched out onto the sidewalk by a mob.

"Wait! Wait!" Jennifer pleaded but couldn't be heard over the commotion. It got worse when the mob from Fifth avenue caught up. Then the absolute worst when Miguel Camacho stormed from the building. Her swollen eye only made matters worse so no one was trying to hear anything she was trying to say.

The man was practically breathing fire as he stomped towards the scene. The younger man at his side swung a large revolver in his hand. Buddha and Rip were both strapped but neither could reach their guns with all the hands holding them in place.

"Yo..." Buddha began but the man beside Miguel shoved the pistol right into his mouth. The 'click' of steel on teeth could be heard. He pressed further, causing him to gag on the barrel. "Argh!"

"Not here Giggles!" Miguel cut in just before a tug on the trigger emptied Buddha's brains onto the car. "Take them to the roof!"

"No papi! I..." Jennifer was calling out but still couldn't be heard over the angry mob of men.

The men worked for him not her so his order was obeyed. The men pulled Buddha and Rip's guns from their pants and drug them inside the building and up to the roof.

"Come on Jennifer," Esmeralda insisted and pulled her daughter away. Murder was a messy business that the women didn't need to see. Jennifer pulled away and followed the mob up to the roof. She had witnessed a few murders but needed to prevent this one.

"What are ju doing in my daughter's car!" Miguel demanded. Buddha tried to explain but the gun barrel on his tonsils made speech difficult. "Take it out!"

"Ack! Bruh, you chipped my tooth!" Buddha complained as if it were the most of his problems instead of the least. He rubbed his tongue along his teeth to be sure. "The fuck yo!"

"Shoot him Giggles!" Miguel decided and the happy man happily stepped up to do just that.

Giggles got his name honestly since he always had a smile or smirk minus mirth, and a perpetual case of the giggles. The happy demeanor was incongruent to the malice in his soul. Even if murder made him even happier.

"Wait damn it!" Jennifer insisted as she worked her way through the mob. She positioned herself between the gunman and the condemned man and spoke up. "Papi, he saved me!"

"He saved us!" Rosalinda cosigned but Giggles was trying to get around her to take the shot. He was a shooter and that's what shooters do, shoot people.

"Tanqilo!" Miguel ordered but still had to pull Giggle's hand down. He turned back to his daughter for an explanation. "Tell me exactly, what happened?"

"We went over to the Bronx. To see a show. You never let anyone give us weed so we stopped to buy some," she said, assigning some of the blame to him. "We stopped in the park on Jerome and..."

"Jerome avenue?" Giggles asked with a rare grimace. He

was a dangerous dude but even he wouldn't stop in that park at night. Few things wiped the grin from his face, this was one.

"Si," she nodded and continued. "Then, some puta madre jumps out and hits me! Snatched my chains off my neck!"

"My poor baby!" Esmeralda moaned of the deep welts on her neck from where the chains were snatched.

"Then, then..." Jennifer tried to continue but the weight of the words held her tongue and she couldn't get them out. The anger was suddenly replaced by sorrow for how close she came to being raped. A chill swept through her body that made her visibly shiver.

"He said he was going to rape us!" Rosalinda added. She added herself too even though Black Rob said no such thing. Jennifer may have been a fine, young stallion but Rosalinda was more on the rounder side of life. An extra plus size, plus she was pretty generous with her vagina so she would have probably given it up willingly.

"Where is he?" Miguel demanded from his sobbing daughter. "The man who touch ju, what does he look like?"

"Still in the park," Buddha finally spoke up. A few men moved to rush over to the park once they got his description. "Black dude. Skinny, hole in his head."

Ten of the men took off in search of this man with this hole in his head. That's exactly what they would find when they reached the Bronx. In fact, dude might be there until sometime tomorrow since dead mufuckas weren't exactly a high priority. This is New York after all and niggas get shot every day B.

"He killed him for us Mr Camacho!" Rosalinda cheered while Jennifer was comforted by her mother. "He saved us!"

"Por que?" Miguel asked curiously. Buddha didn't speak

much Spanish but knew those words from all the time he spent around Rip. Rip's mother was always asking why, since he was always doing shit that would make a mother ask, why.

"Cuz, I'm not gonna stand by and let a chick get raped B. Whether I know her or not. That shit is wack B!" he responded. The response got a nod, followed by more words in Spanish that got him and Rip released. The men holding him instantly let him go the second the command left Miguel's mouth. That was the first time Buddha got a glimpse of real power. He blinked at how quickly his word was obeyed. A few dudes around the way had juice but this was power. Real power that gave life or death like a Pharaoh.

"Ju have honor. I like that. That will take ju a long way," Miguel said, still nodding in thought. He owed, but what could compensate for what he saved. He kept a few thousands in his pockets at all times but they would be an insult to his daughter in comparison to what they saved. "Bente..."

"Come on," Rip beckoned and fell instep behind the man.

Miguel owned every apartment in the building but kept his private residence on the top floor of the walk up tenement building. Just more insulation from whatever could come his way so everyone was slightly surprised when that was where he led them. Most of his workers never stepped foot inside the apartment that housed his family. They wouldn't tonight either since Giggles closed the door on them when he stepped inside.

The well lit apartment gave Jennifer the first good look at her savior. Enough to register that he looked good as her mother ushered her into her room to tend to her wounds. Miguel plopped down on his recliner and pursed his lips at the two young men. He nodded at Rip and decided. "Boricua?"

"Si," he agreed and named his family's hometown back in Puerto Rico. He remembered his friend didn't speak Spanish and switched to English out of loyalty. That too got another nod from the man. He nodded some more before making a decision. He knew Buddha was the leader even if Rip didn't so he directed his question to him.

"You know something about cocaine?" Miguel asked as Esmeralda led Jennifer through the living room, into the kitchen to find a steak to put on her eye. Miguel not only listened for the answer but watched the Buddha's eyes as his women walked by. He noted they never glanced at his women even if one of his women glanced at him. Jennifer just wanted another look, to lock him in. She owed him too.

"Uh..." Buddha paused, which meant no, he didn't. He was a weed peddler and never handled any coke. Dudes on 164th had a booming crack spot but they stuck to the weed. Still his head nodded ahead of a, "Yeah, hell yeah."

"Hmp," Miguel huffed and turned to Giggles. He rattled off directions in rapid fire Spanish that propelled the man out of the apartment. They waited in an awkward silence until he returned a few minutes later. He placed the two kilos of pure cocaine on the table and stepped back. Miguel waited for a reaction and got none. "Small token of my appreciation."

"What we owe you for it?" Buddha asked before moving. He may not know much about it but knew it had value so he would figure it out.

"Ju already paid for it," he nodded and placed a hand over his heart to show his sincerity. Each one picked up one of the bricks but Rip still had another question.

"What about our toolies?" Rip asked. They came with guns and wanted to leave with them. Again, this is New York and niggas get shot every day.

"You mean, the same gun ju just killed someone with?" Miguel asked, making it sound as dumb as it sounded. Even Buddha looked confused since he planned on dumping the gun in the Hudson himself.

"Nah, we good," Buddha confirmed and looked towards the door. They were ahead and he knew that's when to quit. He never knew his dad so he learned most of his lessons from the streets. And one such lesson was to quit while you're ahead.

"Where in the Bronx?" Miguel asked and pulled his own gun. The pretty gun caught both of their attention but neither felt threatened by its sudden appearance.

"Highbridge!" they both said with that cocky, Highbridge swag. Understandably since the west Bronx neighborhood did produce the most prolific killer in modern day history called Killa. Along with one of the most prolific urban authors by the name of Sa'id Salaam.

"Here," he said and tossed his personal gun to Buddha. A nod opened the door and they turned to leave. "Come back when, if ju need more."

"Bet," Buddha replied even though he had no idea what to do with the two bricks he already had. They passed by a worried man rushing in as they rushed out.

"What happened?" Pipo asked urgently as he stormed in. Once he got the slip by Jennifer he took one of the girls he met to a motel for a quick quicky. Another nod got the man seized and stripped of his gun.

"Take him up to the roof!" Miguel demanded. Buddha and Rip didn't speak or look back as they rushed from the block.

They hit the subway and headed back uptown to the Bronx while Pipo was taken up to answer for his dereliction of duty.

"What did I ask ju to do?" Miguel asked, rather calmly given the gravity of the situation. Then again he could afford to be calm with Giggles by his side. The man shared his darker complexion along with darker traits and aspirations that had yet to manifest.

"You said keep an eye on them, on her," he replied, matching his calm. Only because he didn't know the girl was robbed and nearly violated.

"So why the fuck..." Giggles barked with a smirk before his boss calmed him with a wave.

"And did ju? Keep an eye on her? My daughter," he continued.

"Yes! We went to the skate rink and I waited outside," he lied. "Something must have happened inside?"

"See, this is why it's always best to be honest," Miguel instructed to the other men in attendance. The lesson would have been wasted on Pipo since he wouldn't be around much longer. "He fucked up. We all do. I respect that. Lies I do not."

Miguel punctuated the sentence with the nod Giggles had been waiting for. A giggle escaped his mouth just as he lifted the gun. Pipo opened his mouth to protest and only made the situation worse. Not because he was going to tell another lie but, Giggles liked putting pistols into people like Pipo's mouth.

'Gawk!' he gagged loudly when the tip touched his tonsils. The gag was nowhere as loud and the crack of the nine millimeter on the roof of his mouth. A tug on the trigger caused a large crater in the top of the man's head.

A mist of blood and brain hovered in the air as Pipo went

down. He was pretty much as dead as one can get but Miguel wasn't quite satisfied. Another nod got what was left of the man drug over to the front edge of the roof. They usually threw bodies off the back side into the alley but some points have to be made louder than others. About as loud as the thud when Pipo's shell landed on the sidewalk.

CHAPTER 3

"You got weed?" Denise asked, well demanded as she stuck her head into her son's room. His room was in her apartment so she took liberties like that. In fact had he been out or asleep instead of just staring up at the ceiling she would have helped herself to a couple of trey bags. He would complain but she would resort to reminding him about the nine months she carried him. Then, his twelve hour labor complete with how her vagina had never been quite the same. That last part always won since no son wants to hear anything about his mother's vagina.

"Huh?" Buddha asked since his mind was elsewhere. He ran his tongue over the chip that could be felt but not seen and remembered the gun shoved in his mouth. That sucked but the maniacal grin on Giggles face still gave him the shivers. No one should be that happy about killing someone.

Which brought him back to the first body of his life. He was on his way to many more murders but Black Rob was the first. You're not officially a killer until the second or third but they were coming. Especially once he figured out what to do with the two kilos of cocaine in his closet. He had to stash them since Rip's mother was a coke head. She would have sniffed it out and sniffed it up if he kept it at his house. It was an odd blessing that Buddha's mother was just a pothead.

"Who got you all twisted up like that baby?" Denise wondered. Being a mediocre mother didn't mean she didn't care. She did, just didn't know how to be a good one. His father certainly couldn't help since he was murdered shortly after knocking her up.

"Who?" he asked since he only heard the question mark in her tone, and not the question. Still, he had an answer that would let him go back to his thoughts without interruption. "You want some weed? Top drawer."

"Oh, I know where it is," she laughed. The joke was on her though since he only left it in plain sight to prevent her from a search that might turn up weapons or cash. She grabbed two bags before deciding on a third. "Thank you my baby Buddha!"

"Just Buddha!" he called after her to remind her that he had outgrown the pet name she gave him as a baby. He was a fat baby with chubby cheeks that reminded her of a Buddha statue.

"Ok baby," she cooed happily since she had some weed. She may not have a job or a man but she had some weed, so life was good. The doorbell rang and Buddha knew she wasn't going to answer it.

"Fuck," he grumbled since he was content sitting up in bed, rubbing the tip of his tongue over his first war wound. He had been in fights and battles but always gave the scars and stitches. This was his first but would not be his last. Buddha knew exactly who should be ringing the bell so he merely pulled it open in passing and headed into the kitchen.

"That other night was wild B!" Rip exclaimed almost happily. Maybe because he didn't get a gun shoved down his throat. The Camacho crew shoved guns in his face but that's different than in your mouth. Buddha heard the click of steel against his teeth in his sleep. He headed straight through the living room and out onto the terrace while Rip made a pitstop in the kitchen.

"Mmph," Buddha replied as he guzzled orange juice straight from the carton. He put what was left back in the fridge and joined him outside. Rip lit a thick blunt and took a deep pull as they both looked over the block their building overlooked. They could see clear down Ogden avenue one way and up to the bridge Highbridhe was named after the other direction.

"Crazy," he finally concurred. Both turned when they spotted Rip's mother hail a car and hop inside. She didn't have cab fare so it meant she was going to turn a trick. Not a rabbit out of a hat either. Someone was about to get their dick sucked in exchange for financing her next trip over to a hundred and sixty fourth street to buy a rock. Crack was sold in the projects too but they had bigger vials two blocks over.

"Projects doing numbers. Mia's brother just copped a nice anchor!" Rip declared. Buddha had a project chick who had a brother who was slinging crack rocks over in the projects. The buildings had plenty of customers of their own but a hundred and sixty fourth street was booming.

"Shit, if we set up shop on one six seven we would catch all the traffic coming down the hill?" Buddha asked even though he was already sure. That's where they sold most of their weed without stepping on any toes. It was unclaimed territory but since it was adjacent to their building they had the most rights to it.

"Yeah, but we don't know how to cook, or cut, bag, nothing!" Rip whined about their dilemma. Both spotted the bright red car as it circled the block. They both knew who it belonged to and rushed to investigate.

"Come on!" Buddha shouted and tore through his living room. If any of the many local jack boys saw the sweet lick they would bite off more than they could possibly chew. Especially that lunatic Giggles and his big gun. He bypassed the elevator and rushed into the staircase. He and Rip took the sixteen flights of stairs in two leaps all the way down to the lobby in less time than the elevator would have taken.

"Fuck!" he complained when he realized he didn't have his gun.

"I'm strapped!" Rip offered. Not that he could read minds, he just knew how his friend thought. Most times that is, because Buddha could be hard to read sometimes.

A gun wouldn't be necessary at the moment since the local Herbs from his building were the first to accost the pretty, new face with the round, fat ass. A large pair of shades covers her shiny black eye. Later in time they would be called nerds but in this era, in this city they were Herbs.

"Un-uh! No thanks!" Jennifer declined like a pro as the dudes shot their best shots. They realized they were shooting blanks when her eyes lit up her smile as she looked beyond them. "There he is!"

"Buddha gets all the girls!" a Herb protested and stomped off with his head down.

"Sup ma? What you doing around here?" Buddha asked as he approached.

"Ju! I came to help ju with jour problem," she said and

reached back into her car. Both sets of eyes locked in on the Gloria Vanderbilt jeans. They could be as expensive as they wanted, but it was asses like that that made them worth the money. She came up with a shopping bag and looked up at the massive structure they called home. "Which one ju live in?"

"On the sixteenth floor," he revealed even though his mother was home at the moment. He wasn't sure why he answered honestly since he had no idea why she was here.

"We can go to my crib," Rip offered since his mother was already working, so to speak.

"The Bronx..." Jennifer remarked as she looked around on the way inside the building. It was right next door to Manhattan but had a different look and feel to it.

"Yeah," Buddha replied and stole glances at her ass. As round as it was he knew it came with a lot of drama. A deranged daddy with a psychopath sidekick is a lot of drama indeed.

"Nice lobby..." Jennifer rambled about everything she saw on the way up to the sixteenth floor since Rip lived directly across the hall. His apartment faced the back side which gave them a view of University Homes projects.

They could see over Harlem all the way to Jersey but rarely looked past the projects. Both had a chick in both their own building as well as one in the projects. The close proximity didn't matter since project chicks didn't always kick it with girls from the White building.

"Boricua," Jennifer nodded definitively the moment they walked inside. The smell of sofrito and all things Puerto Rican reminded her that he was one. Rip rattled off something in Spanish while Buddha noticed she didn't compliment the apartment when she walked in. After a glimpse of the fully loaded apartment she lived in he understood why. Instead she hit the kitchen and began unloading the bags. "Ju have a pot?"

"What's all that?" Buddha asked as Rip retrieved a large cooking pot.

"Uh, we are not making arroz con pollo papi!" she laughed and went back into the same cupboard he got it from and came out with the right size for the project. Only then did she look up and answer Buddha's question. "Everything you need. Now, where's the perico?"

"The coke?" Buddha asked even though he understood the term. He just didn't understand why she was asking. It was still tucked away in his closet since he still didn't know what to do with it.

"When papi asked if ju knew something about cocaine this one looked shook and ju was all, 'uh, uh, uh,'" she laughed as she came out with jars of baby food. "Plus, ju ain't come back for more so I know you don't know. I'm here to show ju!"

"Um," Buddha hummed and looked to his partner for his opinion. Rip shrugged so he turned and stepped across the hall. A few moments later he returned with one of the kilos.

"Muy bueno!" Jennifer sang happily when she saw the package was unopened. That meant these two weren't sniff heads like many of the dudes on her block. Even her own parents partied hard with the hard drug. The drug simply made too much money to be good for human consumption. Plus, she had seen the violence it induced and knew it was a byproduct of the devil.

"You gone eat this?" Rip asked of the baby applesauce jar since she dumped the strained peas in the sink.

"Eww," she grimaced and he took it as a no. He quickly

scarfed it down and rinsed it out as she had done. Soon each had an empty baby food jar in front of them. Jennifer donned a pair of gloves and wrapped a bandana around her mouth.

"What's this for?" Buddha asked when she handed them the same apparatus.

"Because, it gets into ju pores when you touch it. And into jour soul if you breathe it," she warned. That was enough for them and they quickly suited up like her. Only then did she open the brick and place an ounce on the triple beam scale

"Ok then," Rip announced once he and Buddha had done the same. Once they had measured out the right amount of baking soda they began to cook crack. Ounce by ounce until half the kilo was transformed. They moved the cooked batches to the rickety dining room table to dry.

"Next lesson!" Jennifer announced and dumped a bag of tiny vials on the table. So many, they spilled over into the floor.

"Green?" Buddha asked of the colored tops. Most of the empty crack vials in the parks and staircases were red. Others were blue from the projects, but no green.

"Si. Alejandro and his crew uses rojo. Ju want jour own color for jour own product," she explained. Rip tilted his head curiously but Buddha's nodded since he understood. It was just like the little Buddha figure stamped on their bags of weed that distinguished their weed from the competition. Unfortunately in identified the regular weed they sold instead of the better weed sold around the hood. Still, two blunts for three bucks was a good deal. Plus it was a brand and black folks love brand names.

Rip and Buddha stole glances at the pretty girl rambling on as they filled the vials. They shared a mutual, 'you see this shit' look at the mountain of vials stacking up. They ran out of vials before they ran out of crack. The rest went into another bag for another time.

"How much are these?" Rip asked to his partner's relief. Buddha was wondering the same thing but was shy to ask the girl.

"In Harlem five bucks. Here, ten," Jennifer replied. Both nodded even though neither understood why just yet. The truth was a matter of supply and demand. Harlem had more junkies and plenty of drugs so the price was cheaper.

"Why you doing all this?" Buddha had to ask as they wrapped it up.

"Because, ju have honor. And I like that," she replied just as her father had. In an underworld full of criminals, honor was rare but respected. She had written her number down before she left home but finally handed it over as they left the apartment. "Call me..."

"I'ma call you," he smiled and nodded as she got into her car. He rubbed his tongue on his chipped teeth and thought about Giggles and all the guns. His head shook from the truth, "I'm not fucking with you ma."

"Word! Now let's go shoot some ball!" Rip agreed as they went back inside to change to play ball. Neither knew it yet but once they started slinging crack their basketball days would end.

❀

"A-yo!" a voice called out behind Buddha and Rip as they headed over to Nelson park to play some ball. Both heard the call but neither responded until they heard their names. "Buddha, Rip!"

"Sup yo!" Rip demanded aggressively when they turned and saw who was calling them.

Black Bob was Black Rob's older brother and twice as fucked up. Black Rob was definitely a piece of shit but his brother was the asshole that shit him out. His sidekick Tone-Capone was by his side like always. The two terrorized bodegas and numbers spots all over the borough of the Bronx. Neither Buddha nor Rip had much money on them since they were on their way to play ball but were still on alert. Neither was strapped for the same reason. Most people who get caught lacking get hit in their own hood. The comfort level makes them relax and go out without protection.

"I'm saying yo. You heard my brother got hit up last week on Jerome ave?" Black Bob asked and lifted his chin defiantly.

"Word, that's fucked up B," Buddha offered contritely. Not only had he heard it, he heard the shot that put the city out of Black Rob's misery since he fired it.

"Y'all be down there selling bags in the park," Tone-Capone stated matter-of-factly since it was a well known matter of fact.

"And?" Rip pressed and cocked his head to see where they were going with it. Meanwhile his mind instantly replayed the decision to leave his gun in the top drawer. He vowed to never leave home without from then on, if they made it from then on.

"And y'all ain't see shit yo? Ain't see my brother down there?" Black Bob dared.

"Hell naw. Shit was booming since Rick and Doug were in the house. We sold out and hit Forty deuce," Buddha shrugged. There was a tense few seconds that seemed like minutes while Black Bob decided if he wanted to believe it or not. It certainly sounded believable but someone had to pay for his brother's death.

"A'ight B," Bob nodded menacingly and spun on his heels. He wasn't sold either way but it was midday on a busy street. Wrong place, wrong time. "Let me find out..."

CHAPTER 4

"What now?" Rip asked as he and Buddha stared at the large bag filled with tiny vials. At ten bucks a pop it represented nine thousand dollars more than they ever had at one time in their lives. Thus far they had only ever had a combined thousand bucks between them both. It went for more of the mediocre weed they sold.

"Now we hit the block!" he cheered and explained the plan. It was their plan even if he came up with it on his own. Not to mention Rip didn't quite get it.

"I still don't understand why we would just give this shit away?" Rip asked again but the answer was the same.

"Cuz, no one knows us for crack. No one knows this spot," Buddha said as they posted up on their corner. Alejandro had a hundred and sixty fourth street and the projects had their own dealers. The corner on 167 and Ogden ave was unclaimed and cut off traffic coming down the hill. Not enough to step on toes but brisk enough to establish themselves.

"A'ight B!" he relented but twisted his lips to show what he thought of it. A couple approached so he handed them a free tester apiece.

"What's this?" the woman asked as she inspected it.

"Coke?" her companion asked as he inspected the vial. Neither used coke but it was free in a city that takes more than it gives. The recently married couple both worked at Yankee stadium but walked down the hill to save money. If they saved enough money they could afford to have kids. Then a house in the suburbs to raise them.

"We just smoke weed," the woman replied and began to give it back.

"Mix it with your weed," Rip suggested and turned to the next person coming down the hill. The couple shrugged and tucked them into their pockets and went on their way. They would mix the crack with their weed when they got off work that night. Once they inhaled the devilish drug they would exhale all their hopes and dreams along with it.

"Free tester! Cracks!" Buddha announced as he passed out the testers to all passersby who passed by. A pack of young teen girls saw the traffic and came to investigate.

"What is that?" one asked while her friends checked out Buddha up close. They all giggled and posed while he paid them no attention.

"Nothing for you shorty," he replied, frowning at them before turning away.

"He ain't all that!" One huffed and marched off. Buddha may have discriminated on who he passed them out to but Rip didn't. The sooner they passed off the designated two hundred vials the sooner they could make some money.

"Here, here, here..." he said five times to each of the five teens as he gave them each a tester.

"Let me get two?" a familiar voice asked as Rip worked.

"Hell naw ma!" he fussed and turned away from her.

"Sucker!" Rip's mother Alva fussed and stomped off. Luckily for her quite a few of the men who received the testers didn't use. They did have dicks though and gladly exchanged the free rocks for some free head.

"Welp..." Rip sighed once they handed out the last of the free testers. "What now?"

"Now we get paid!" Buddha smiled. By the time they returned with a hundred more vials the customers were waiting. Some returned for more free crack but gladly spent since they now had to pay.

Weed sales took so long to generate a thousand dollars they would have spent half of it before ever seeing a thousand. Today was a different day and a different product. An hour later they had a thousand dollars between them. Life as they knew it was about to change.

※

"A-yo B, this shit is mad crazy son!" Rip exclaimed excitedly as he flicked through a handful of cash.

"Word!" Buddha agreed because it was. They could see customers still roaming around the gas station from their bird's eye view. "We're going to need some help."

"True..." Rip replied and squinted to help him think. They had a few dudes in their crew from the building so he mentally ran through them. His head shook and nodded through the process of elimination. "Monte, Joey, E-baby and Big Hank."

"Joey steals," Buddha quickly reminded. He didn't immediately reject their kleptomaniac friend but put it in the air.

"Shit, ain't nothing to steal! Money rolling in so fast he should be good!" he countered. Buddha's head nodded as the next question came to their minds. "How much to pay them?"

"Mia said Mike gives his crew fifteen bucks off a hundred," he recalled. His semi girlfriend from the neighboring projects had a brother who controlled the flow of most drugs in University Homes housing projects. They had just recently moved to the quickly emerging crack trend but he paid the workers the same twenty percent.

"Sounds about right," Rip quickly agreed. It wasn't long ago since they were getting twenty off a hundred to sell weed, until they saved up enough for an ounce and went solo. He went to the phone to summon some of the crew while Buddha yelled down from the terrace to collect the ones who were out front.

A few minutes later the selected few of the larger crew were all assembled in the living room. They vibed to Wu-tang on the radio as a thick blunt circulated two puffs and pass style. Once the weed was all hovering above Buddha dumped a bag of vials on the table in front of them. The teens looked at the drugs, then up to him for explanation.

"Son, where y'all got these shits from!" Joey cheered and fondled the vials. Buddha locked in on his fingers to make sure he didn't cuff any. The kid was like a magician when it came to making shit disappear.

"Where don't matter. Now y'all tryna get this money or what?" Rip barked like a boss. Buddha had other ideas on how to play it so he cut in.

"We caught a plug. He paying twenty off a hundred," he began, then paused to let that digest. A quick scan of faces and he knew who was who. E-baby looked excited while

Monte looked slightly shook. Big Hank was doing the math in his head to see how many vials would buy the latest Jordans. Joey was scheming as usual.

"Word B! Shit popping!" Rip cosigned and tossed a wad of cash on the pile of drugs. Joey's shifty eyes quickly counted it before it even settled. He could count money still in a person's pocket.

"Shit, so I sell five hundred worth and I get a 'huned?" E-baby asked, tilting his head skeptically. Not that he didn't believe, he just believed it was too good to be true. His last summer job for the city barely paid a hundred bucks a week to shovel garbage. And New York city garbage has got to be the worst garbage in the galaxy. In the course of the summer he had found a hand, a head and two whole babies.

"Sell a thousand and get two hundred!" Buddha cheered since he saw the money moved him.

"I'm down!" E-baby shouted and locked it in. Big Hank heard all he needed to hear and nodded in agreement.

"Me too!" Joey announced and all heads turned to Monte. Buddha opened his mouth to dismiss him since this was no time or place for hesitation. The streets move too quickly for slow thinkers.

"I'm down," Monte reluctantly agreed a second before getting excused. Buddha still had reservations but kept them to himself. One day he would recall this exact moment.

"One more thing!" Rip announced with an urgency that got everyone's attention. He looked around to make sure it was undivided before continuing. "Don't sell my mom's shit! Not a fucking crumb! Word to my muva, don't sell her shit!"

"A'ight, no doubt, word, got you B," the teens agreed and nodded. If all that stood between them and getting money was not selling to a crackhead, well that hurdle was hurdled with Olympic ease.

"A'ight. We are not all selling at the same time," Buddha decided. "Once you two sell out the next man is up."

"Word," Rip agreed as he collected the vials Buddha had dumped on the table. They weren't counted so no one knew Joey managed to steal four of them. He was quite the thief with the dexterity of David Copperfield.

"A'ight, E-baby and Joey up first," Buddha decided. They counted out fifty caps apiece and handed them over. Rip and the rest came out to direct traffic and keep watch for police. It was only a couple of hours before the men switched positions. By the end of the day the crew had hundreds of dollars in their pockets and were hooked for life.

"Just the man I was looking for!" Ms Alva sang happily when she ran into Monte in the staircase. Crack head or not the woman was still good looking and still had a fat ass. Still, as in not for long because crack addiction demands your body and soul. It literally doesn't let you keep shit but your name.

"Me? Rip is up the block," he replied since he wondered why Rip's mother would be looking for him.

"I know but I'm not looking for him. He won't give me nothing!" she pouted angrily since her son refused to give her any crack. It was tough love but only caused her to work the streets to get it anyway. Rip might have fared better just feeding her a daily supply of dope. Instead she sucked dick and took back shots in staircases to feed that habit.

"I can't sell you nothing man!" he fussed and tried to walk

off. Monte was happy his friends put him on and had strict instructions not to sell the woman anything.

"I ain't got no money no way!" Alva laughed since she never had money for long. "Let me suck your dick for one?"

"Naw, I..." he began to decline until he registered all the words. The short, stubby teen didn't get any pussy so the offer stopped him dead in his tracks. He wasn't sure if he heard her correctly so he sought clarity, "Huh?"

"Let me suck your dick for one?" she repeated before registering the twinkle in his eye. "I mean, two. I'll suck it for two."

Luckily for Monte she didn't go to five because his dick was rock hard from hearing the offer. So hard his vision got blurry and he had trouble getting it out of his jeans. He had to unbuckle his belt and let them fall to his ankles. Then grab the handrail when his dick disappeared into her hot mouth. He would remember this blow job just as every man remembers their first blow job. Meanwhile, this was her third of the day.

"Fuck!" Monte grunted as his knees buckled from the sensation. Practice makes proficient so Alva was damn near perfect with her head game. She sucked, stroked and hummed until she felt him begin to twitch. That was her cue to throw it into overdrive and snatch his soul.

"Mmhm," she hummed and nodded as the pulses filled her mouth with salty semen. She clamped down tighter and swallowed with loud gulps that won his heart. By the time she stood she had both his heart and soul. She extended her empty palm to be filled. "Let me get three baby."

"Shit," Monte grunted to himself after she scurried off to smoke her compensation. He had lost half of his virginity and nearly called her back to get the rest. His head shook it off when he remembered what he was supposed to be doing. He fished out thirty bucks from his own pocket and moved it to the money he had to turn in from sales. Both he and Alva knew this was just the beginning.

"You a'ight?" Rip asked when Monte returned. He looked both relaxed and guilty at the same time. Nothing takes the edge off like a good blow job but he felt guilty that it was his friend's mother. He shouldn't have since she was a real mother sucker who tricked for treats like everyday was Halloween.

"Who? Huh? Nah, yeah..." he stammered. Luckily two customers rushed up with the urgency of crack heads and stole their attention.

"Lemme get two," one said while shifting from foot to foot in anticipation. The incident was quickly replaced by the flow of sales. Business was so good they ran through the first batch of cooked coke in a few days. Now it was time to cook up on their own.

"That's everything," Buddha nodded at all of the supplies laid out on the counter.

"Yeah," Rip cosigned even though he didn't know for sure. He was far more interested in Jennifer's round ass when she was demonstrating how to cook. He wasn't going to let his friend know that so he stepped forward to take the lead.

"One more thing!" he remembered and pulled the bandana up, over his mouth and nostrils. Rip rolled his eyes at the extra precaution since he was the reckless type in everything in life. He drove without a seatbelt and fucked without a rubber. Cooking coke without a mask was more dangerous than both combined.

"Word," he sighed and pulled his up as well.

Both men measured cocaine and baking soda. Then filled pots with water on the stove. The coke went into the baby food jars with water. Rip made sure to lag a second behind to make sure he did what his friend did. He still did something wrong somewhere.

"Ah yes!" Buddha cheered like Jay-Z after copping a deuce fever IS, fully loaded.

"Fuck!" Rip declared since he fucked his up somewhere, somehow.

"Damn B?" his partner protested at the cloudy water in the jar. The lost ounce left nothing to lose so Buddha dropped some more baking soda into the jar and gave it a mix. A sense of relief swept through the small, galley kitchen when it began to rock up. It was short lived when the front door swung open.

"What you in here cooking?" Denise asked when she walked into the apartment.

"Nothing!" Buddha declared and rushed forward to block her from entering. Except there's no such animal as telling a black woman where she can go and can't go in her own house.

"Move boy!" Denise fussed and moved him aside. She squinted and Rip with his mask, then down at the crack drying on paper towels. There was a moment of silence as she processed what she was seeing. Her era called it 'Free base' but she wasn't concerned with her son cooking it in her kitchen. What she wanted to know was, "You got weed?"

"Yeah," Buddha quickly confessed and pulled his personal

weed from his pocket. His mother cuffed it just as quickly and hurried back into her room to blaze up.

"Wish I had your mom's B," Rip heard himself say before he could stop it. It was out so he left it there and measured out the next ounce. The spot was booming so they needed to get more work for their workers.

CHAPTER 5

"Yo B..." Buddha exclaimed. It was all he could get out since the stacks of cash on the table took his breath away. Before this week he had never held a thousand dollars. Now he had ten thousand of them.

"Word!" Rip cosigned since he felt the same way. Another feeling quickly chased that one away. "I'm about to go fuck something!"

"By something I assume you mean Yvonne?" Buddha laughed since his friend was wide open on the acne faced teen with the banging body. She lived a few flights above them. Rip had hoes in different area codes but nothing beats that around the way girl who lets you beat her back out at will.

"Like you ain't going over to the 'jects to fuck Mia fine ass!" Rip retorted and cocked his head in a dare to deny it since she was his around the way girl who let him beat her back out whenever he wanted it.

"Word! Got me a three pack of Jimmy hats too!" Buddha laughed some more. He laughed even harder at the face his friend made at the mention of a rubber. Knowing good and well his dog planned to go raw dog.

They dapped each other up and went their separate ways. Rip only had to bound up a few flights of stairs while Buddha had to make a quick stop at home. He never carried his pistol in his own building, but always carried it when he left. He intended to pop in and out but his mother had other plans.

"Hey ma," he greeted as he entered. The plan was to breeze in light and leave out thirty eight calibers heavier. The chrome pistol Miguel gave him was a pretty nickel plated piece of art but it barked and bit like a big dog.

"I need to talk to you," she said and patted the empty spot on the sofa beside her.

"Need weed?" he asked and dug into his pocket for the blunt he had for him and Mia to blaze before they boned. He hoped it was just weed since his mind was set on some pussy.

"Well, yeah..." Denise laughed and accepted the weed even though it wasn't what she wanted to talk about. "But, what are you doing with that stuff baby?"

"I sell weed. You know that?" he wondered. She patted the sofa again so he huffed and puffed before sitting.

"I'm talking about that free base. That stuff ain't no joke!" she warned. She would know since she and Rip's mother Alva used to be best of friends. They both tried the new drug at the same party. They both got high as fuck but she was the only one who made it back. Most of the people from that party were still smoking crack a year later. Some would hit their version of rock bottom and stop. Others were gone for good.

"I know ma. You know Ion use nothing harder than reefer," he reminded. Denise nodded at what she knew and felt relief. "We just selling that stuff cuz we got it for free. Once it's gone we're done."

"Just promise you'll be careful!" she insisted. Buddha had to laugh since he was only here for the protection of his pistol and prophylactics. He couldn't tell her either so he just snickered and stood. "It's not funny boy! I ain't tryna lose anyone else I love!"

"I know ma," he comforted and sat back down to pat her hand. He too had lost a few people he loved and some of them were still living. Plus the father he would never know because the streets ate him before he was born. That only fueled his ferocity out in those same streets. "Trust me, I'm good out there in these streets!"

"That's exactly what yo pops said the last time I saw him," she sighed and drifted into her own head. She was so far gone she hadn't noticed her son left until she heard the door close behind him. The blunt in her hand gave her a nudge so she put a flame to it and took a pull.

"Who dat?" one of the project teens asked as he saw a figure approaching through the dark. He reached for the pistol in his waist to make it darker for the intruder if he didn't check out.

"That nigga Buddha!" another teen practically cheered when he was illuminated by one of the few remaining lights. The residents shot out some of the lights to create a buffer zone at the entrance. Buddha was good in the projects in general because he was cool. Then specifically because he was a star on the basketball court as well.

"Sup Capo," Buddha cheered back and began a round of daps and pounds all around. "What's good up here yo?"

"Chillin B, getting to this cheddar!" the teen who nearly pulled his gun proclaimed and pulled a pile of cash from his pocket. No sense getting money and not flashing it from time to time.

"Word," Buddha replied and nodded since he had a few piles of money himself. He got to keep his unlike the kid who had to turn his over to Kevin. He could feel the eyes above and looked up to see Mia looking down at him.

"Mmhm," she hummed and turned back to the TV. It was enough for Buddha to give another round of daps and pounds before heading upstairs. He took note of the brisk flow of customers flowing through the courtyard . The projects were self-contained and had enough customers to get rich.

Buddha took one last breath of semi clean project air before entering the pissy project stairwell. The stench of stale urine and sex acts could literally take the breath away. The combination of odors actually made the temperature rise ten degrees.

He took the four flights by leaps and bounds so he wouldn't have to breathe until he reached the fourth floor. Once he did he exchanged the old breath for a new one and headed to the end of the hall. Mia knew he was on the way up but he still had to knock on the door. He twisted his lips into a 'yeah right' when he saw the light from the peep hole.

"Sup B," her brother Kevin grunted when he pulled the door open.

"You!" Buddha exclaimed when he saw the new dookie gold rope chain around his neck. A large anchor swung in the middle of the Coogi sweater he wore. "You doing it like that!"

"Just like that!" Kevin laughed as the teen checked out the rest of his outfit. The Bally sweatpants may have been Dapper Dan but the Bally shoes were the real deal.

"You here to see him?" Mia quipped from the sofa. She liked to be the center of attention so she stood and marched down the hall to her room.

"Ion know how you do it," Kevin laughed. He knew his sister was extra everything and he wouldn't have put up with any of it. His new found wealth came with some new found females so he headed out to seduce one.

Buddha let out a sigh before heading down the hall to Mia's room. She was definitely extra but the pussy was extra good and that's exactly how and why he put up with her. She was busy yapping on the phone when he came in.

"Mmhm..." she hummed with an eye roll when he reached over and rubbed her legs. She pretended to ignore his touch but still spread her legs a little more. She yapped it up until he reached the promised land in her panties. "Girl, I gotta go."

"Naw, you can keep talking," Buddha laughed but she hung up anyway. He pulled his hand away and went for the blunt he brought along with him.

"We should roll up a woolie!" she suggested with the enthusiasm of picking a ride at an amusement park.

"A what?" he reeled like he didn't understand. Woolie blunts were the latest craze around the hood but he didn't find anything amusing about mixing crack with his weed. Which is why he wouldn't hit any blunt he didn't personally see rolled up.

"A woolie! These shits be making me horny!" she purred

and rubbed his crotch. There are no more prophets to come but it was a glimpse into her future.

"Naw B. Ion fuck with them shits yo," he said forcefully enough for her to drop it. For now since her brother had stacks of bags of crack vials in his room. She could help herself to a few and he would never miss them. "Plus, I make you horny!"

"Whatever," she hummed when he reached back between her legs. She spread them a little more so he could work his fingers beneath her panties. He did, and lit the blunt with his free hand.

They smoked and kissed while the blunt went around and she soaked his fingers. It got clipped halfway through in favor of some fucking. The couple managed to strip while maintaining their lip lock. The only pause came when he reached for a rubber to wrap up the wood.

"You and them things!" Mia said and shook his head at the condom. He was the only one of the other ones she was fucking who wore one. He knew she fucked other dudes which was all the more reason to wear one.

"Cuz, I ain't tryna have no little Buddhas no time soon..." he replied as he worked himself inside. Promiscuity would one day take its toll on her vagina, but not this day. He grimaced as the snug, hot box sucked him inside.

At this age, young Buddha had one position and one speed. He braced his feet on her footboard while she gripped the sheets. The sexual equivalent of buckling their seatbelts. Once they did it was off to the races. She moaned and made faces while he groaned and grimaced. They had three rubbers all night, and they used them all.

CHAPTER 6

"Twenty Gs B!" Rip proudly proclaimed when he finished a second count of the cash. That was after paying the team and still had plenty coke left. "We need to shop B!"

"We need to re-up," Buddha said thoughtfully. Rip was ready to spend but he was already thinking long term. The first couple kilos were free but they would have to pay from there out.

"Son, we got a whole 'nother brick! Let's get fresh!" He shot back. The rest of the crew already had new shell toes and Levis. It was time they spent a little bread too.

"Yeah, I guess we could spend some..." Buddha agreed and contemplated how much he was willing to part with. It came down to just how fresh he intended to get. Rip helped the decision along and passed him half the cash.

"Ten Gs apiece," he said. He liked the sound of it so much he had to say it again. "Son, we got ten Gs apiece!"

"We need to hit Fordham road," Buddha acknowledged. If you wanted to get funky fresh in the Bronx it was the place to go. Usually that required a bus down to Yankee stadium, then the D train up to Fordham. They would do no such thing with ten thousand dollars in their pockets. That much cheddar meant catching a cab. "Gotta swing by the crib first B."

"Word!" Rip agreed emphatically since leaving the block meant toting some heat.

Buddha intended to get his gun but also tucked five of his ten thousand dollars away into his stash. He nodded with his decision to save half of what he made from then on out. Joey and Monte had spent every penny they made as soon as they made it. The money came so easily it was only right to spend it just as easily. Growing up without enough affects different people in different ways.

Some like Rip and Joey wanted to floss and front. Broke was the norm so they spent as much as possible to return to being broke as quickly as possible. Others like Buddha and E-baby intended to never be broke again so they stacked their bread. Denise was posted up in the living room when he walked inside. She greeted him with her normal greeting.

"You got..."

"Here ma!" Buddha cut in and handed his mother a bag of weed before she could finish. He paid no rent or utilities so he couldn't complain about supporting her weed habit.

"Thank you baby!" Denise called after him as he went to tuck the cash in the stash spot and his pistol in his waist.

"Yeah," he said on his way back out of the house. He caught up with Rip out front, chilling with Joey.

"Yo, let me go with y'all B!" Joey pleaded as soon as Buddha emerged from the lobby. He always wanted to go with them since he never had any money. Even now since he had spent all of his earnings already. Plus, he stole. He had been getting them into shit by stealing shit for a decade.

"I already told him nah!" Rip protested hotly. He noticed the crew kept deferring to Buddha like he was the boss. They had done so for years but it was starting to get old.

"Shit, then it's nah," Buddha shrugged at the simplicity of it, like a boss. Politics came naturally to him so he knew to protect his friend's ego. An unchecked ego is more dangerous than any tsunami or hurricane.

"Shit, at least let us get some work while y'all balling out!" Joey grumbled. It had been Buddha's suggestion that the crew only sold while they were out. Too much could go wrong without them on the scene. No telling what the sticky fingered kid would steal without supervision.

"Wait til we get back. Gotta cook up," Rip answered as Buddha hailed a gypsy taxi. The Oldsmobile 98 pulled to stop and let them in.

"One sixty first?" the driver assumed since most of his fares were up and down the hill to the train station.

"Yeah, nah," both men answered at the same time. Buddha declined so Rip turned to hear why.

"Take us to Fordham road," he said and killed the driver's impending protest with two twenty dollar bills. Being paid up front cut the risk of them dodging the fare once they got where they wanted to go.

"Bet!" Papi behind the wheel cheered and collected the bills through the slot in the bullet proof partition. CREAM by the Wutang clan came on the radio with perfect timing. The perfect soundtrack for their first shopping spree.

"Cash rules everything around me, cream, get the money!" Buddha rapped his best Method man voice.

"Dollar bill y'all!" the driver added all the way uptown. He let them out at the top of Fordham road and the Grand Concourse. They had been here before, lots of times, but never like this. Never with more than a couple hundred apiece their mothers gave them for school shopping. Now they had Gs to spend of their own.

Never with pockets stuffed with thousands of dollars. Never with the choice to buy whatever they wanted. They looked down the block trying to decide which way to go. What to buy first.

"Un-huh! Yup, that's it!" Rip declared when his mind was made up by the flashing sign above a jewelry store. He took the lead and marched off down the hill. The dookie chains and Cuban links in the window sealed the deal.

The elderly Jewish store clerk reached for the pistol behind the counter when he saw the two young goons enter. He released the gun when he saw the familiar look in Rip's eyes. The lustful gaze of a black man ready to buy some gold. That look paid for his homes, cars and put his four kids through college, law and medical schools. And the black men, well they got their gold.

"How can I be..." he tried to ask but Rip already made up his mind.

"That's it! Right there!" he insisted and pointed at a thick Cuban link chain with a large medallion hanging from it. Buddha laughed as his friend bounced like a child waiting to get on a ride at the amusement park.

The door had to be buzzed open for them to get out so the clerk didn't mind hanging the chain around his neck. He pushed the countertop mirror close and knew he had him. Rip nodded at his reflection and reached into his pocket.

"How much!" he demanded, ready to pay whatever it was.

"For you..." the clerk asked and sized him up. Different

people got different prices based on what they looked like they could pay. Hymie had seen his share of dope boys and guessed by the shell toe Adidas and Levis these guys were new to the game. He would have gotten as much out of them before one of the two inevitables came to claim them. Dead or jail and neither needs new jewelry. Plus he couldn't tax them so much they would go to any one of the many other jewelers on the block.

"Hook me up B!" Rip pleaded as he contemplated how much to charge for the couple hundred dollars worth of gold.

"Five thousand. And I'll throw in the bracelet for another grand!" the man cheered like he was doing him a favor. Meanwhile, the studious Buddha sat back and studied both sides of the deal. Both added to the life lessons he studied daily.

"Bet!" Rip agreed and happily parted with over half of his cut from the fledgling operations. A stark contrast to Buddha leaving over half of his at home.

"What about you my friend?" Hymie cheered again since he wanted to do Buddha the same favor.

"I'm good," he shot back but still looked over at a diamond studded medallion. It was half the size of the one Rip just bought but looked twice as expensive. "For now."

"Ok, you guys come back! Anytime!" he solicited on their way out of the store.

"Let's hit Dr Jays! I need some kicks!" Buddha declared. He wasn't ready for any bling but was definitely in the mood for some new kicks. Everyone has vices and his was fresh sneakers.

Buddha noticed being noticed as they headed down the block. Females jocked but then again that was everywhere he went. It was a pair of shifty teens locked on them from the time they stepped out of the jewelry store. Rip was oblivious to the potentially dangerous situation since he was too busy admiring himself in every window they passed. Or admiring every round ass that passed them which was plenty on a Saturday on Fordham road. The gold around his neck and fools gold in jeans had him utterly distracted.

"Come on..." Buddha insisted and pulled him around a corner.

"What up B? Them chicks was jocking!" he grumbled as Buddha literally snatched him into a pizza shop. "If you hungry just say..."

Rip was rudely interrupted when Buddha pulled his gun just as the curious youths came around the same corner. They looked around for their intended prey until they realized they were now the prey. It was loud and clear when Buddha rushed out and shoved the gun in their face.

"You following us yo?" Buddha demanded and pressed the gun to his nose. The kid let out an audible gasp and went for his waist but Buddha beat him to it and snatched his gun away.

"Chill B! You got that!" the kid pleaded. He looked even younger up close but a gun against your nose will do that.

"Chill 'nuffin yo!" Rip shot back once he caught on to what was going on. He pulled his own gun and searched the other kid but he was unarmed.

"You was gonna stick us up with this B?" Buddha laughed at the rinky dinky little revolver. Obviously the gun had a sense of humor and got in on the joke as all the bullets fell out. The kid twisted his lips in embarrassment.

"We should wet this nigga!" Rip growled and slowly squeezed his trigger. He looked up and down the block to see who was about to see a murder. It would be his first and he was eager to catch up with his partner.

"Chill B," Buddha said and let go of the kid's shirt. He stayed put since he didn't want to get shot in his back. "What's yo name kid?"

"Trouble!" he shot back proudly. His mother, teachers and grandmother kept telling him he was nothing but trouble so he embraced it.

"Sure the fuck are! Where you from Trouble?" he asked and gave Rip a nod that sent his gun back into his own waist.

"Jerome ave," he explained which explained a lot. Most of Jerome ave was run down and grimy so he had to get it like he lived.

"You wanna make some cheddar? Come through the white building and look me up. Ask for Buddha," he said and turned to leave.

"Can I keep my burner?" Trouble asked.

"Nah. Come through..." Buddha replied over his shoulder. He tossed what was left of the gun into the trash and finished shopping.

CHAPTER 7

"Damn B! Y'all doing it like that son!" Joey cheered when Buddha and Rip hopped out of yet another gypsy taxi. The smile on his face contradicted the timbre of jealousy in his throat. Even his black eyes glistened with envy as he scanned their bags. The shifty kid tried to guess how much they spent on their shopping trip.

Buddha had secretly hoped the crew wasn't out front when they returned for this same reason. It was as futile as hoping the whole building was gone because one rarely saw the building without the same faces hanging out in front of it. For good reason though since one's hood is one's safety zone. An oasis of comfort in a dangerous city. Which is why some people tucked their chains under their shit when they stepped off their own block.

"Yoooo! That shit is ill B!" Big Hank declared of Rip's new chain. He cheesed proudly since this was the very reason he bought it. All eyes took in the Cuban link, then shot over to Buddha to see his. Monte looked confused, while Hank looked disappointed. Only E-baby nodded like he got it since he didn't plan on spending his on frivolous shit either.

"Y'all ready to set up shop?" Buddha asked for a couple reasons. One to make back what he just spent, and two to change the subject from their shopping spree. He was never particularly comfortable with all eyes on him. The look in Joey's eyes made him even more uncomfortable.

"Hell yeah! Word! Bet!" they all agreed since the money was just as addictive as the dope the fiends smoked in their pipes.

"I'll go get some G-packs," Rip said and followed Buddha into the building.

"Thought y'all had to cook up..." Joey murmured under his breath. He could use it as an excuse for some fuck shit but he was just plain shady from the jump. Any excuse would suffice. Seeing what they spent only added fuel to the fire in his desire.

A few minutes later the workers had work and the spot came to life. The junkies had begun to check with them before hitting the projects or one hundred and sixty fourth street. Their dope was better since they were still too green to whip it into an inferior product. Now that they were back out business was booming.

"I need to use the bathroom,". Monte suddenly declared.

"Piss in the corner B!" Hank demanded since he had just peed there himself.

"Gotta do number two," he said and rubbed his tummy as proof. Buddha once again reaffirmed his thought that the kid wasn't about this life. He was always a part of the crew so he was out here with them but Buddha knew he shouldn't be. Especially not saying shit like 'number two' when he had to take a shit.

"Handle your biz B," Buddha said, giving his permission. He twisted his lips and watched the kid twist away. He saw Miss Alva fall in behind him and squinted at the coincidence. A slight commotion stole his attention away from Monte over to Joey and a customer.

"This ain't like the last one I got!" she complained and held up the vial he just sold her.

"Same shit! I..." he protested in the high pitched tone Buddha knew well since he knew him so well. They had been friends since first grade and his voice went back to first grade whenever he lied. So, Buddha heard the tone daily since not a day went by that he didn't lie about something. He leaned up from the car he was leaning on to go fix whatever was broken but Joey changed his tone, literally and figuratively and swapped out the vial for another. "Here! Fuck outa here!"

"You good?" Buddha asked anyway. He tilted his head and pursed his lips like Arnold did when he needed to know what Willis was talking about.

"Hell yeah!" he shot back and went back to serving the flow of customers.

"Hold it down for a sec," Buddha called over to Rip who supervised from the other side of the parking lot. Four eyes were better than two but curiosity was getting the best of him.

"Gotta take a number two!" Rip called after him and cackled. Buddha tried to keep a straight face but that shit was funny so he couldn't. He was still smiling from the joke as he entered the lobby.

Buddha made his way over to the elevators and pressed the button. A second thought changed his mind and directed him to the stairwell. One side went up above while the other went down to a locked fire exit. It was an unofficial motel for kids who lived with their parents. He had smashed a few there himself so he had to take a peek.

'Un-huh' Buddha laughed to himself when the sounds of sex greeted him before he could turn the corner. He was right but it still took a few seconds to process what he was seeing.

"Ssss, mmmm, mmhm..." a female moaned in reply to the quick, short, choppy strokes Monte was delivering. Buddha wanted to turn away but the weed in his system suggested he stay and watch. Plus he was proud that his nerdy friend finally got some pussy.

"I, I, Ugh! Argh!" Monte grunted and groaned as he bust a nut. Buddha snickered proudly and pulled back so he wouldn't be seen. Until he heard a familiar voice that pulled him back.

"Let me get three yo!" Miss Alva demanded before dude could get his dick out of her. Two of the three people present turned towards the screech and all eyes fell on Buddha.

"You buggin the fuck out son!" Buddha barked for a variety of reasons. First was fucking their mans moms. That's something you just don't do. And no one should have to tell you, 'yo don't fuck my moms', but Rip did tell them. A lot of people fucked his moms since she started smoking crack but not his boys. "There are millions of females in the Bronx, fuck them, just not your mans moms."

"Huh?" Monte asked in reply to the first reason. Then came the second when he had to pay up. He had no choice but hand over the two vials he agreed to part with to purchase the pussy.

"Son! The fuck!" Buddha snapped as he parted with the

drugs he was supposed to be selling. His money was always right and he quickly found out why.

"I pay for them with my own money," Monte explained sheepishly. He proved it by removing his twenty off the hundred from one pocket and placed it in the other pocket with the crew's bread.

"Still B, Rip would kill you if he caught you fucking his moms B!" he sighed. It was a bit of an exaggeration he hoped but Rip would definitely kick his ass for this infraction.

"Yo, y'all be getting all the ass and bragging, and..." Monte sighed. He didn't finish but didn't need to since his friend felt his pain.

"Still yo, don't fuck dude's mom. There's plenty pussy around here B. Fuck one of them," Buddha sighed. Once again he knew he was in over his head. He was the leader so it was up to him to save him before he drowned. "Now you gotta go tell Rip what happened."

"You for real!" Monte reeled wide eyed with fear, just like Buddha knew he would.

"Nah, I'm fucking with you. Let's go get something to eat..." he laughed. The look of terror in his eyes was sufficient enough to shut this down.

※

"Yo, I got eight bucks. Hook me up?" a junkie named Robert pleaded as he came upon the dope boys holding court in the project's courtyard.

"Fuck outa here yo! We not taking no shorts B!" Lil Bam laughed dismissively and dismissed the loyal customer. Loyal or not the boys didn't do customer appreciation days or sales since any shorts came out of their cut. Already cut short since Kev was shorting them by only paying them fifteen dollars off each hundred they sold.

"But you hooked Tanasia up for six bucks last night!" he recalled and was about to regret it.

"Dats cuz she sucked my dick for the other four!" the teen shot back with a wicked cackle. No one wants to hear about their wife sucking dick for any price, let alone four dollars. The husband and wife team had begun smoking a year ago. Both maintained their jobs and habits for as long as possible but crack is a jealous god. Like all other false gods it demanded their loyalty and full attention.

"You hurt unc feelings!" Zero laughed as the crack head slinked away.

"Damn base heads ain't got no feelings B! They smoke them shits away," Bam shot back hotly. He was the son of one so he knew first hand. He was lucky that his mother took her show on the road and didn't roam around the projects.

"Here come Kev," Zero announced as the boss exited his building. Kevin stopped and looked around the courtyard before stepping over to his workers.

"Sup?" he asked and looked around some more. The average eye wouldn't be able to see any difference but his wasn't average. Something was amiss even if they missed it.

"Cooling B. Err thing crisp," they both answered. The conversation paused to serve two junkies who came up.

"Let me get two," the first one asked and presented a well worn twenty dollar bill. It was a classic 'cop and go' as it should be. The next was the classic junkie shit they dealt with on a daily basis.

"Yo, wanna buy a VCR-ra?" the man asked and retrieved the unit from under his shirt like a magic trick in reverse.

"The fuck is a VCR-ra!" Kev cackled and set off a round of

laughter. This junkie didn't have any feelings left either and didn't give a fuck about getting teased for not being able to pronounce the letter R without the extra ra. He wanted a hit and that's all that mattered at the moment.

"I'm saying yo, this shit is brand new. Just give me two, three. Three rocks," he bargained.

"Fuck we look like Blockbusters or some shit!" Kev barked.

"Fuck outa here!" Bam demanded and stood. The crack head turned to leave but was a little slow so the teen gave him a swift kick in his ass to help him along. The trio cracked up for a moment until Kev got back to business.

"Business slow yo," he nodded. The receipts had been slipping for a few days so he came out to see why.

"Yeah, it is," Zero agreed. He got paid twenty dollars off each hundred he made since he was the supervisor but he still felt the pinch in his pocket. All eyes locked on a good spending customer named Michelle. She was still fine enough to have dudes spend money on her which she used to fuel her new habit of smoking woolie blunts.

"Fuck she going?" Kev asked as she breezed through the courtyard without even glancing their way. No one could answer so he got up and followed from a distance. Her jiggling ass made following fun but he was more interested in where she was going.

"Sup yo. Let me get something for eight," Tanasia asked as she came over to the bench.

"Bitch we just told Robert we not taking no shorts today!" Zero barked.

"Word? He just told me y'all asked me to come," she replied.

"Word? Come on, I got them other two bucks for you..."

Lil Bam said and took her into the stairwell for a two dollar blow job. No feelings indeed.

Meanwhile, Kev walked behind Michelle as she strolled out of the projects. She headed over to Ogden avenue which meant she could be going literally anywhere since that's where the bus ran. It went down the hill to Yankee stadium and the train station that linked the Bronx to the rest of the world. She didn't though and stopped short at the gas station where the Buddha crew had set up shop.

"Sup Michelle, I got you!" Joey cheered when he saw her and rushed forward to serve her.

"Hell naw, your shit be short yo!" she fussed and bypassed him in favor of Big Hank. "Let me get five."

"Shit, you can get six..." he said and wiggled his eye to express the sex in his mind.

"Nigga I can get twenty if I want!" she shot back hotly. She may have tricked with ballers and shot callers but didn't trick for drugs. Not yet anyway because this drug wasn't like the other drugs. She may have just smoked her crack laced in the weed for now but that's how most start.

Everyone locked onto her ass as she walked over to the bodega for the rest of her get high supplies. She had a couple trey bags at home and now had some base to lace. Now all she needed was some White Owl cigars and Pink Champagne to sip on.

"Hmp," Kev hummed when he saw what he needed to see. He had no problem with anyone selling anything anywhere other than his projects. Now his customers were leaving the projects to cop and that could very well be a problem. His head nodded with his discovery as he headed back into his domain. Something would have to be done so he went to contemplate what, exactly that was. Meanwhile, Buddha had a question of his own that needed answering.

"Yo, Joey. Fuck she mean, yo shit short?" he asked and made his way over. He caught Kevin's back as he walked away but thought nothing of it.

"Bitch bugging yo," he shrugged and pulled out his pack of crack vials from his left pocket. They were exactly as he and Rip packed them so he didn't see any problems either. His shoulders shrugged too and life went on.

Joey went back to serving the regular and new customers who copped and went. Every now and then he slipped his hand into his right pocket and produced one of the shorter vials. The slight difference allowed him to skim a small amount of rocks from each vial. It added up over the course of days and weeks.

❀

"Man you ain't really going over there? To Highbridge!" Manny pleaded as Trouble stomped forward. The heel of his right sneaker flopped with every step and made him even more determined.

"Hell yeah! That stick up shit is gonna get us killed!" he warned. They had already been shot at enough times to know one day someone was gonna shoot straight enough to hit them. Plus, New York is a big city in a small world. People will see you again and if someone you robbed sees you, before you see them you might not ever be seen again.

"So? At least we eating!" his friend shot back. The pain of having to risk his life to eat was evident in his voice but some of that pain was from not having a choice. He certainly didn't choose to be born in this city, to this borough, to a crack addicted mother he hadn't seen in years.

"Son look like they was eating pretty good. I'ma take my chances with them..." Trouble declared and came to a stop at the mile high steps on 167th street. Most people do just to take a look at the daunting climb ahead. He stopped to ponder what lay ahead. Up that hill was a whole new world that could play either way.

If Buddha put a bullet in his temple for trying to rob him it would be justice. He nodded at that possibility, then shook it away. The Off track betting spot on 161st was always packed with people trying their luck. He was too young to enter so he took that first step to try his luck with Buddha.

"Fuck that shit B! I'm Audi five thousand!" Manny spat and spun on his heels. He would stop in the first store he saw and steal his breakfast. Fuel for the busy day of robbing and stealing that lies ahead.

Curiosity and hunger propelled the kid up the stairs in no time flat. Buddha took his pistol which meant they went to bed hungry last night. Nothing motivates a man like hunger or hate. Not even love. He looked around for a moment, then set off towards the iconic White building.

"Yo B, 'member me? I tried to stick y'all up on Fordham road," Trouble practiced as he went over the few blocks. He winced at how that sounded and shook it out of his head. He sighed and settled for a, "Sup yo."

He got his chance sooner than later since he could see Buddha posted up at the gas station as he neared Ogden ave. The brisk traffic reminded him of the many drug spots on his block. Still, he couldn't tell if it was weed, coke, crack or smack until he got closer. The unmistakable look in a customer's eyes answered the question for him. The empty look in a crack addict's eyes goes right down to their soul.

"Sup yo," Trouble greeted as he practiced.

"A'ight then," Buddha nodded as he instantly placed the face. When someone pulls a gun on you, you better remember the face. "You ready to get some bread?"

"And meat," the kid laughed even though he was serious. The turkey and cheese hero Buddha was eating made his stomach growl loud enough to be heard. "What I gotta do?"

"Sit here and watch for 5-0. If you see any coming from either way, what you gonna say?" he asked and cocked his head like it was a dare.

"Uh, 5-0!" Trouble shot back using the citywide slang. It actually stemmed from the cop show Hawaii five-O but they didn't know, nor cared.

"Exactly," Buddha said and stood so the kid could take his spot. It came with half a sandwich too since he heard the kids stomach. "Finish this for me. I'm full."

"Bet!" Trouble cheered. People had lost trust, loyalty and dignity over a few bucks but Buddha had just secured his for half a hero.

CHAPTER 8

"That's him there chica!" Rosalinda vowed when Jennifer's phone began to ring. The girl had just been pouting because the hero thug who saved them hadn't called yet. Dudes she hadn't even given her number to blew her line up all day but the one she wanted to call still hadn't.

"I knew he would!" Jennifer declared as if she hadn't just been whining about Buddha not calling. She let it ring a couple more times just to play hard to get, before cooly picking up the receiver. "Hello? Huh? Who? The fuck!"

"Not him I take it?" Rosalinda chuckled at the disgust on her face when Jennifer slammed the phone down on some booty beggar.

"Dudes may as well have a cup and sign will beg for booty!" she huffed. Luckily for Rosalinda her mother summoned Jennifer before she could go off on another rant. "Coming mami!"

"Ju ready for our hair appointment?" Esmeralda asked. She was certainly ready, dressed to the nines and dripping in diamonds.

Miguel glanced over the sports section in his hand to make sure his daughter had enough clothes on. He literally hated summer time once his daughter filled out since her fillings were always spilling out of her clothes. He gave Rosalinda a look over before ducking back into the paper to see what his Mets were doing.

"Si mami!" the spoiled girl cheered. Hair appointments usually came with shopping and dinner so she was definitely down. "Can Rosalinda come?"

"Not fair for her to sit hours waiting on jour hair," the woman replied. The good excuse allowed her the private mother/daughter time she was after anyway. She knew there would come a time when her daughter had no use for her so she enjoyed her while she could.

"I'm fine. Have some stuff to do at home," Rosalinda quickly replied.

"I'll drive," Giggles offered like he had a choice. Pipo lost his job along with his life so the hired hitta had to drive the boss's wife around. He had ambitions beyond just driving and shooting people like Pipo but would play his position until a better one came his way.

"My bag!" Rosalinda remembered as they all headed out of the apartment. Esmeralda and Jennifer didn't need to wait on her so they didn't. She smiled and waved as the two left the apartment and headed back down the hall. She bypassed Jennifer's room where her bag was and entered the spare bedroom. Miguel sat his newspaper down and followed her inside.

"Ay Dios mio!" He declared and bit his bottom lip as the teen began to peel off the painted on jeans. Truth be told his wife was just as fine if not finer but cheating never is about looks. It's about lust, lack of integrity and licentiousness. Most of all about different pussy.

Rosalinda giggled at the compliment and finished getting undressed. She sat on the edge of the bed as he came over and unzipped his pants. A second later she had a thick dick in her face. It didn't do either of them any good in her face so she opened wide and took it inside her hot mouth. The dick stifled the next giggle that came when his knees buckled. Being a young, chubby teen and having this power over a powerful man wasn't lost on her. He was rich and powerful with an army at his disposal and all she had was a pussy. A tight, furnace of a vagina but just pussy nonetheless.

"Shit!" Miguel fussed and grimaced at the hot mouth working him over. He reached between her thick legs and found an even hotter vagina. He fondled it until it soaked his finger. Once he squeezed that finger inside the blow job was abruptly canceled. "Lay back..."

"Si papi," she cooed, then hissed loudly when he shoved himself inside. Now, Esmeralda may have been just as fine if not finer than her but her pussy hadn't been this tight in a decade.

"Shit!" he repeated because a good, hot, tight pussy makes dudes say that. He took one of the big nipples in his mouth and began to suck as he humped. He slowly grinded in the teen until he felt his balls begin to bubble. He now had a dilemma to deal with. Nutting in Esmeralda at this age got him a wife and daughter. He didn't want another of either so he quickly snatched himself out. "Open!"

"Aghgh!" Rosalinda grunted and grimaced as her mouth filled with salty semen. The firm grip on her head gave her two options. Drink or drown, so she swallowed in loud gulps.

"¡Muy bueno, excelente!" Miguel moaned when he pulled his rapidly deflating dick from her mouth. You know it's some good sex when you switch languages in the middle of it.

Rosalinda giggled again as he wobbled on rubbery legs when he pulled his pants up. The pockets were filled with cash so he pulled out a roll and peeled off a few hundred.

"Por que?" she asked so she wouldn't feel like a prostitute. The good sex and thrill of sneaking around was it's own reward. She didn't want to get paid for the pussy.

"For looking after my daughter all the way," he replied. Honestly since he didn't pay for pussy with any one other than his wife.

"Oh, ok. No problem. She's my best friend," she said and took the money.

"No, I am your best friend. You tell me whatever she does, whether she likes it or not!" he reminded. Rosalinda nodded since she had been doing just that. Jennifer knew she was a double agent and kept some things to herself. The girl could only report exactly what she wanted her father to know.

"He likes ju," Esmeralda snickered at Giggles behind the wheel. She caught him glancing back at Jennifer every chance he got as he navigated the dense Harlem traffic.

"Who mama?" Jennifer asked and looked out both windows. She secretly hoped to see the black kid who saved her brown ass but he wasn't on either side of the street.

"No, him," her mother laughed as Giggles blushed under his brown skin.

"Mama!" Jennifer reeled in embarrassment for him as well

as herself. Giggles was no doubt a handsome fellow. He had that same dark skin as her father, chiseled into a picture perfect face. If anything he was out of her league since he was a few years older than her. Plus she had seen him with some drop dead gorgeous boricua mamis over the years.

"What ju are a beautiful girl!" Esmeralda reeled. She was already fucking at that age and had no doubt her daughter wasn't far behind. The tight reigns they kept on the girl would only go so far, for so long. And once she got some dick in her wild horses couldn't keep it out of her.

"Thank you mama!" she cheered at the compliment. She had been feeling quite the opposite since Buddha still hadn't called her. She glanced up at Giggles in another light just as he looked up at her in the mirror. They shared a moment just before he rolled into the back of a car.

"Shit!" he fussed at the fender bender and hopped out. He and the other driver quickly assessed their fenders and shook their heads. This was New York city where people played bumper-cars with real cars. There was no damage so no need for police, tickets or insurance claims. They hopped back into their cars and continued on their way.

The ladies got their hair laced while Giggles waited outside. Ever the hustler he made connections with the local Spanish kids on the block. He was thinking about expanding as soon as Miguel put him in the game. In fact he had ambitions far beyond being a driver and shooter for the man. No, he wanted to be the man himself. He was a natural shortstop and knew from experience to play his position. That's what he would do, for now.

"Hello?" Jennifer asked since she didn't recognize the number on the new caller ID box. The privileged girl had her own line so it could only be someone she gave the number to but she didn't recall it. Most of her days and nights were spent on the phone with her girlfriends since her overprotective parents didn't allow boyfriends.

"Can I speak to Jennifer?" Buddha asked as politely as possible in case her mother answered. He also took a little of the natural bass out of his voice since it made mothers think a grown man was calling for their teen.

"Who is this!" she demanded hotly, even though she recognized the voice immediately. This was the call she had been waiting for since giving him her number a couple weeks ago when she taught him how to cook coke. This was the call she had been hoping every other call was. She wasn't going to let him know though.

"Gar, uh Buddha," he corrected after almost giving his given name. His own mother didn't call him Garik anymore so neither would she.

"Mmhm!" she hummed, which meant, "Why haven't you called me since I gave you my number a year ago!"

"My bad, I just wanted to call, um, yeah," he stammered since he still wasn't quite the ladies man just yet. He did well with the girls in his hood since they practically threw the panties at him since he turned fifteen. "A year tho?"

"Why ju just now calling! I gave ju my number last fucking month!" the fussy diva fussed like fussy divas fuss. She was more glad than mad to hear his voice so she quickly got over it. "So anyway, what's up?"

"Yo, we're done with all that we cooked up. Anyway can you come show us how to do it again?" he asked believably.

WE RUN NEW YORK

To him anyway since Jennifer didn't buy it. He repeated everything she taught and picked it up instantly. She cooked up the first two ounces and he did the rest. Even coached Rip through his like an old pro.

"Jeah right!" Jennifer cackled and stood to admire herself in the mirror. "Ju know how to do it just fine. If ju want to see me, say that!"

"I want to see you," he shot back immediately. Always the quick learner he learned just that quickly that chicks like dudes to take charge. So he charged. The truth was he had been thinking about her when he had time to think. Life had been moving so fast that it wasn't very often. The crew needed to re-up so he could kill two birds with one stone. "I'm going to take you over to City Island!"

"Sammy's? I love Sammy's!" she cheered and bounced in the mirror. Even she liked watching all that good titty meat heave up and down. Twerking hadn't officially been born but women have been shaking ass and titties since the beginning of time.

"Uh..." he began since he never went into any of the more exclusive spots on the Island. He and his mother always frequented the lower priced spots further down the block. He looked over at the pile of money on his dresser and changed his tune. "Sure. That's a bet."

"When ju coming to pick me up?" she blurted before thinking it through. Buddha wouldn't make it inside the building if he came on her block to pick her up. By the time he parked her father's people would be all over him. She cringed at the thought as he replied.

"I ain't got no car ma," he replied and looked back at the money. "Not yet anyway."

"No problem papi. I'll pick ju up. Friday?" she suggested.

"Friday is good, great," he said and smiled through the line. She heard it and smiled back before they said their goodbyes.

"Friday! We're gonna run out of work by Wednesday!" Joey exclaimed since he heard his side of the call.

"Nah, we'll just slow down a bit. Let other niggas eat too before it's a problem," Buddha sighed. Mia relayed the message that Kev wanted to speak with him so it could only be about the growing number of project crack heads coming to cop. Buddha never heard of market research or demographics even though he studied it in real time in real life. He saw more and more customers from the projects everyday. Handled wrong that could be a problem.

"Fuck them niggas! They don't want no static with us!" he proclaimed and picked up his pistol to prove it.

"A'ight killer," Buddha laughed and stood. The light hearted laugh twisted his friends lips when he took it the wrong way. Buddha had beat him to catching a body when he shot Black Rob so he took it as a dis. "I'm about to go see what Kev talking about, then fuck the dog shit out his sister."

"Word. About to get my dick wet too," Rip switched gears and laughed. They were young enough to brag and laugh about their sexual conquest. Plus, neither had yet to meet a chick they cared about enough not to. They dapped and departed to their different destinations. Rip arrived first since he was just going up a few flights.

CHAPTER 9

"Come in!" Yvonne called from the sofa so she wouldn't have to get up. She left the door unlocked once her mother left to work the night shift at Lincoln hospital.

"How you know I ain't no rapist!" Rip fussed as he entered the unlocked apartment.

"Cuz, I give you the pussy. Fuck you need to take it for?" she asked and sat up straight to share the sofa with him.

"True that," he cosigned and put his feet up on the table since he saw her mother leave an hour ago. He was the man of their house when she wasn't home. He never would have tossed bags of weed and cigars on the table if her mother had been home. "Roll up!"

"I want a woolie blunt baby!" she purred when she didn't see any crack in the pile.

"Them shits stopped my dick from getting hard last time!" he protested before he could remember that last time wasn't with her. "I heard..."

"Mmhm, yeah nigga," she shot back and twisted her lips.

Wasn't more she could say beyond that since she fucked other dudes. "Well, let me smoke one. I'll clip it so you can smoke after we fuck."

"Ok..." Rip nodded and pursed his lips like he liked the sound of that. After all it did include getting high and getting some pussy. What more can a ghetto kid ask for?

"Yay!" Yvonne cheered and did a happy crack dance when he pulled a few vials out of his pocket. Her and her crew used to get a few woolie blunts out of each vial. Now she crushed the entire contents of a whole vial for the first blunt.

Rip watched almost lustfully as she moistened the cigar with a mini blow job. Ironically his mom was giving Monte a whole blow job in the stairwell. She saw him watching and gave a girly giggle. The show was over and she got down to business. She emptied the tobacco and laid out the weed. Then laced the crushed crack along the length. Making sure to concentrate a few extra crumbs at the tip for that soul searching first pull.

Rip licked his own lips when she put the blunt in her mouth. His eyes went wide when the orange flame tickled the tip. He found himself inhaling with her as she took that first long, sizzling pull. Even holding his breath with her as she held the noxious smoke for as long as she possibly could.

"Damn ma! You hold your breath longer than Aqua man!" he laughed. It was a good laugh even though he wanted to snatch the blunt and take a pull himself. He refrained since pussy was still the priority at this point.

"You stupid!" she laughed but didn't laugh long since she was holding a smoldering woolie blunt in hand. Her legs moved and helped Rip stay focussed on the prize between her thighs. If not he would have taken a hit and killed his chance to hit. Once she was good and high she wanted some dick in her.

Luckily the strong weed and even stronger cocaine got the teen higher than their building stood above Ogden avenue. She outed the blunt and spread her legs as he ran his hand up her thigh. Her box was gushy wet when he got there.

"Damn ma!" he marveled at her slippery lips. He ran two fingers in and out of her as she soaked them with juice.

"That shit be making me horny!" she grunted and bucked under the sensation. She had neither time nor desire to sit there while he played in her pussy. She wanted no needed some dick inside of her urgently. She lifted her hips to help facilitate the removal of her panties.

"Bout to tear this shit up!" he declared as he kicked his sneakers off and pulled his jeans down to his ankles. The thought of strapping up never even crossed his mind and he pushed into the pussy raw.

"Mmmm," Yvonne moaned and put one leg on the top of the sofa. Her way of calling his bluff his supposed to be tearing shit up. He braced a foot on the floor for support but his sock slipped on the shag carpet. An easy fix when he pulled a Jordan back on one foot and braced himself. He searched around for a stroke and commenced to tearing that shit up.

Yvonne hummed and howled as he humped and grunted. Both had plenty of warning but neither took it since both were pretty reckless. They did smoke crack filled blunts so what's a little unprotected sex. Rip threw the dick into overdrive and drove it home. He leaned all his weight on his and pressed down to the bottom of her box and let one go.

"Fuck! Shit! Arghh! Mmmm," he reiterated as she rubbed

his back. Rip reached for the blunt before he even pulled out of her insides. Once upon a time they spent all night fucking. Now that the fucking was done they spent the rest of the night smoking woolie blunts.

<hr />

Buddha moved through the busy project courtyard with the prowess of a politician. The projects and White building were two separate entities that sometimes clashed but generally kept peace. Their close proximity forced them into the same schools from kindergarten to twelfth grade so they learned to coexist. Intramural Relationships between the two also helped smooth the way.

After dapping his way through the courtyard he entered the pissy stairwell and bounded up in one breath. He heard raised voices as he exited the stairwell onto Mia and Kevin's floor. A few steps verified it was their voices so he slowed and tuned in. He was sent for so he wanted to hear if whatever this was had something to do with him.

"The fuck Mia! I counted my shit man!" Kev protested loudly.

"Ion know what you even talking about yo! I ain't take shit!" she shot back and rolled her eyes. Her eyes rolled whether she was lying or telling the truth.

"Yo, I had a hundred caps in here, now it's ninety!" he insisted.

"Ask ma. She was in there!" Mia shot back. The room went silent with the weight of her blaming their mutual mother for missing crack vials. He just blinked in disbelief while she rolled her eyes and neck. Buddha mistook the pause as a conclusion and knocked. The peephole went from light to dark as it was opened and covered by an eye. A symphony of locks clicked and clacked echoed in the stark hallway before the door was pulled open.

"Buddha bless!" Kev cheered happily enough to make Buddha produce a weary frown. They were never that close to be happy to see each other. Plus he was here to fuck the dog shit out of his sister so he knew he wasn't cheering for that.

"Sup Kev?" Buddha asked and meant it. Most times people ask 'sup' or 'how are you', they don't really want to know. He did though since he had been summoned. He carefully recalled the last few times he was over and was able to definitively rule out Mia being pregnant. Not by him anyway since he took all necessary precautions to make sure that didn't happen. In fact, he had yet to feel the insides of any vagina ever, without a latex barrier. The poor fellow had no idea what he was missing out on. Rip may have been sowing seeds all over the Bronx like some ghetto farmer but Buddha was a virgin when it came to raw sex.

"Nah, I'm saying yo!" Kev laughed and extended his blunt.

"I'm cool," he declined because he didn't smoke weed he didn't see rolled with his own eyes. The woolie blunt era was in full effect and creating a new age of future addicts. A nod from Kevin sent Mia to her room so the men folk could talk. "Sup?"

"I see y'all got some movement on 167," he said and paused for reply. Buddha had none so he was forced to continue without input. "Yeah, so I was thinking. Why don't y'all get on the team! Roll with us!"

"Who?" was the first thing that popped in his head. He

had his own team so why would he want to get down with another team. Still, he was shrewd enough to let the bigger man believe he was the bigger man. Stature has nothing to do with status but Buddha still deferred. "I mean, we ain't really doing it big like y'all. Small time shit B."

"Y'all can tho! Shit I got a connect with Alejandro and them on 164! I'll pay y'all twenty on the hundred. My own crew don't get that!" he relayed.

"I'll spit at my boys and see what they say," Buddha nodded optimistically even though he already knew the answer. The misleading reply sounded better than the stern 'fuck no' it concealed. Plus he still wanted some pussy.

"Bet," Kev stood and dapped him up gleefully as if it were a done deal. All the teens in the projects were clamoring to be down with him so he couldn't imagine getting turned down.

"Yo..." Buddha called before he could walk out. Once he turned back he popped the question on his mind. "Since you got the connect, what does it cost to shop with you? Like, a brick?"

"A whole brick? A kilo?" Kev asked like he wasn't sure what it was. He was, he just wasn't buying whole kilos yet himself. There was plenty of money to be made off the half keys he was getting from a third party, twice removed from the actual connect. He mentally doubled the fifteen thousand he paid for a half, then added his tax on top. "For you, thirty five."

"Word up," Buddha nodded. "For me..."

"Yeah, just get at me when you get yo cheddar up B," Kev shot back with a condescending chuckle. He literally looked down on most people because he was six feet four inches but this was figurative as well.

"Bet. For me," he laughed but for a different reason. He had forty thousand dollars of his own and his partner Rip had the same. He was still smiling about it when Mia came from the rear.

"What he say?' Mia asked as she appeared a second after the door closed behind her brother. She heard the entire conversation from where she was hiding in the hallway.

"Who?" Buddha asked the nipples pressing against the T-shirt she wore. It and the fuzzy slippers were the only things she was wearing and it confused him for a moment.

"My brother is crazy!" she giggled at the tacit compliment. Despite her denials she didn't want him to know she was swiping her brother's drugs to smoke with her friends.

"Oh, nothing. Business," he replied and twisted his own lips as he contemplated how much to reveal. He decided that was enough so he pulled her down onto his lap. She couldn't ask any questions with his tongue in her mouth so that's where he stuck it.

"Mm-mm," she moaned when his hand slid under her T-shirt and found her juicy little juice box. It was good and gushy so he ran his fingers in and out of it. The feeling was so intense Mia abandoned the kiss to moan and hiss. "Damn B!"

Buddha lifted her shirt to suck her hard titties and nipples. The added sensation caused her to moan louder and deeper. Both were amazed and amused when she had her first orgasm in his hand. She gratefully kissed all over his face and mouth. It was his turn now so he strapped up and flipped her over onto the sofa. The position of the sofa allowed him to look down over the courtyard while he dug her out from the back.

It was a good thing her moms still had it wrapped in

plastic since she formed a puddle as soon as he pushed inside. Mia sucked his lips and neck while he pounded the pussy until he went stiff and filled up his Jimmy hat.

CHAPTER 10

"Let me get two?" a woman of an undetermined age asked Monte and extended a twenty dollar bill. It's hard to gauge a black woman's age in general since black doesn't generally crack. That's why some fifty somethings look like twentysomethings. Then along came crack and turned thirty some things into octogenarians.

"A'ight, bet," Monte replied after sizing her up. He enjoyed having cash to spare for the first time in his life. What he enjoyed more was all the pussy and head he was getting on a regular basis. Rip's mother was his favorite but he would trick off on other crack heads if they were fine. This one was far from fine so she could get her rocks and go.

"A'ight," she concurred after checking them over. She looked over at Joey and rolled her eyes since he sold her the short caps the last time she copped from him. There was no time to watch her ass as she walked off since the next customer had walked up. The spot was jumping and the Buddha crew was running out of work.

"Well?" Black Bob asked and Tonya returned to the

basketball court on University that separated the projects from the White building. He and Tone had posted up on a bench where they could keep tabs on the spot without being spotted. Tonya was sent out as a scout and returned with her report. She didn't mind setting people up to be robbed if the price was right.

"They got it going on!" she cheered. It usually took sucking two different dicks to earn the twenty they sent her with to check it out.

"Word," Tone-Capone agreed since people were coming and going at a brisk pace. What was hard to narrow down was when the crew would be out there. There was no set schedule and it was either deserted or wide open.

"A'ight yo. Good looking out..." Tonya said and turned to leave since she had two whole vials and didn't have to share with anyone.

"Hold up ma!" Black Bob called with a chuckle. He robbed for his daily bread and didn't give shit away for free. "Come on up in the staircase and slob this knob!"

"Knobs..." Tone corrected since he wanted some head too. Nothing is free in life, and even less in the Bronx.

※

"How's it going?" Buddha asked when he came around the corner. putting Trouble on a corner as a lookout meant he and Rip were free to do other things. Rip went on shopping sprees and got fresh while he spent hours on the phone with Jennifer before their first date.

"Err thing cool yo," Trouble reported automatically. He had seen Joey selling crack from both pockets but wasn't sure what to make of it. He was observant like that and not much got by him. Monte slipped off twice with Rip's mom but knew tricking was part of trapping.

"Rip been out here?" he asked and looked around again even though the first scan didn't produce his partner.

"Nah B," the kid replied and kept alternating up and down the block. Buddha nodded since the kid was on his job.

"Run up the block and grab me some wings from the Chinese spot," the boss directed and came out of his pocket with some cash. "Get whatever you want too."

"Bet!" Trouble cheered. A little too loud and turned a few heads. He had the right to be happy since he hadn't been hungry since he started coming over to work with the Buddha crew. His handsome face had even filled out from finally getting enough to eat.

Buddha fought the urge to light a blunt and settled for a Newport instead. He was selling drugs and not partying after all so it made sense to stay sharp. He watched the ebb and flow, come and go of the brisk business. A new/used 190 Benz pulled to a stop in front of the gas pump and out came Yvonne followed by Rip. Both were loaded with shopping bags but what caught his attention was the new chain dangling from his partner's neck.

"Word B?" Buddha asked as he came over and inspected the new piece.

"Look what I got!" Yvonne cheered and turned her bumpy face to show off the gold, bamboo earrings in her ear. Her name was laced in the middle, made from more gold.

"Had to lace my girl," he said and got a kiss in reply.

"Baby mama you mean!" she huffed and sashayed across the street to their building. Both waited until she was completely out of sight and earshot before speaking.

"Word B?" Buddha asked with a mix of mirth and incredibility. He shouldn't be surprised since his partner bragged about never, ever using a rubber. This most likely wasn't his first kid and wouldn't be his last. Especially now that he was pushing a Benz.

"I'm saying yo. Nawmean," he explained and turned their attention towards the car. "Papi on Jerome hooked me up!"

"Jerome!" Trouble snickered since he knew most of the car lots and dealers specialized in selling stolen cars known as 'tag jobs'. Cars stolen out of state and swapped vin numbers with similar cars from the junkyard.

"Shut the fuck up shorty!" Rip barked at the kid. He would have murked him and his man on Fordham if he had his way.

"Get back to work B," Buddha said and collected his food from the kid. He nodded at his decision to not just spare the kid, but put him to work when he saw how he devoured his food. Only people who have missed meals eat like that. Feeding him was a source of loyalty blood relations can't even foster.

"Yo, what's up with boricua mami? You hit that yet?" Rip asked as wiped some dust from his car.

"Who? Nah, we're gonna link up soon. We need to re-up and she is the key," he said. She was pretty and thick but so was the piles of cash he was stacking away. Plus, she was probably more problems than he wanted to deal with.

"Hell yeah! Keep this cheddar rolling in B!" his friend replied as he looked over his car once more.

"Word to my mother!" Buddha cheered and looked at his car again himself. He wanted a whip as well but it could wait. It would have to wait until he got his weight up, literally and financially. Miguel told them to come back when they needed more so he technically didn't need the girl. Acknowledging that forced him to acknowledge he just wanted to see her. It was personal, not business.

※

"They definitely getting paid B!" Tone-Capone exclaimed as he and his partner in crime staked out the Buddha crew once again. The stickup kids did their homework on victims before moving on them. His brother Black Rob wasn't as calculated which was why he was where he was.

"Yeah, just gotta figure out how they moving?" Black Bob said since he just couldn't figure it. Most of the other drug spots rolled wide open but these guys kept irregular hours. Some days they might not come out at all. They couldn't nail down a pattern because there wasn't one.

"Should just get them little niggas," Tone growled as one of Kev's young workers ambled by smoking a blunt with a young chick by his side. He was a hater at heart so he hated seeing the youngsters enjoying the money they worked for.

"The nigga live in yo building son!" Bob shot back. He was grimy as fuck but didn't shit where he ate. He didn't rob fellow residents but anyone outside of their projects were fair game. "Might just have to hit up them Puerto Ricans on 164."

"Word!" Tone-Capone agreed. Especially since Alejandro brought in other boricuas from other parts of the borough. Caucasians don't have a monopoly on racism and the fair skinned Puerto Ricans didn't employ any of the local black kids

They had scoped out the booming spot a few times and saw they were way too comfortable. Miguel Camacho's name rang bells across the bridge but not so much in the Bronx. A lieutenant would come around and collect cash every hour and take it up to an apartment in one of the walkup buildings.

A few bucks to one of the crackheads got them the information on which apartment held the cash. It wasn't as easy as just running inside the spot with workers on the street, but walking out would be a breeze. The crew's regular schedule allowed the stickup kids to slide in early the next morning before they showed up and posted up on the roof. They had a bird eye view of the busy cop and go traffic of the drug trade. No one saw them enter the building so they wouldn't think much when they walked out.

"Son!" Black Bob huffed and sucked the blunt smoke deeper into his lungs. Not that he needed to finish the statement since Tone-Capone saw the same thing he was seeing.

The lieutenant had made several trips in and out of the building which meant the money was stacking. He made the mistake of following some young girl into one of the other buildings and the robbers made their move. The ski mask came down as they descended the stairs. They had heard the distinctive knock they used enough times that day to easily mimic it.

'Tap, tap-tap-tap, tap, tap' and footsteps approached from the other side.

"Shit..." the worker inside fussed and paused the porn he was watching. He rushed over and snatched the door open without ever looking to see who it was. Way too comfortable and it was going to cost them.

"Where the dough nigga!" Black Bob demanded as they rushed in on top of him. He only got to look at the fully automatic Uzi they kept for situations like this since Tone rushed over and confiscated it. He didn't answer quickly enough so Bob bopped him on the back of his head and opened a deep gash.

"Puta madre!" the man fussed and touched the wound. The handful of blood helped change his mind about putting up a fight.

"Never mind!" Bob laughed when they reached the living room as saw the neat piles of cash lining the coffee table.

"Fuck y'all got going on?" Tone laughed at the frozen image of a woman with a dick in her face on the TV screen.

"Fuck that shit B! Check for more money and drugs!" Black Bob shouted as he tied the workers hands behind his back, then muzzled his mouth.

"Bet!" his partner agreed and hit the kitchen. A large bag contained hundreds of the red capped vials the crew sold. He grabbed it but missed another one just like it in the cupboard. "Got it!"

"Should off this nigga..." Bob contemplated before they turned to leave. There was no reason to kill him but people don't really need one anymore. Tone had no opinion either way so he shrugged. Bob decided on another whack from the pistol and cracked his jaw. The loud moans served as traveling music as they fled the apartment.

Once out in the hall they slowed and peeked outside. The lieutenant was busy with the young girl and the workers were busy working the brisk flow of customers. The robbers removed their ski mask and casually exited the building, They were barely noticed as they beat a hasty retreat off the block. Just one of the junkies caught a glimpse as they rounded the corner.

Now the race was on to blow the money as soon as humanly possible.

CHAPTER 11

"Jackpot..." Tone-Capone hissed when he spotted the expensive sports car rolling up Ogden ave.

"A bitch too!" Black Bob cheered when he saw a female pushing the whip. The stickup kids immediately moved on their unsuspecting prey. Jennifer may as well have been a gazelle grazing in the Serengeti as she bobbed her head to the banger on the radio. Meanwhile, two male lions crept from different angles to ambush her. She had just parked and reached for the door handle when they arrived.

"Sup B?" Buddha asked as he appeared around the corner just at the right time. Highbridge is one of those places where residents have to wait on their guests for an escort. The would-be robbers stopped in their tracks when Jennifer got out and hugged Buddha.

"Hey Buddha!" Jennifer cheered and squeezed his neck while the dangerous drama played out around her.

Black Bob and Tone-Capone took a few more steps while deciding if they should press on or fall back. Buddha just smirked at the irony of two brothers dying over the same car. He slid a hand around to his gun while the other found that sweet spot in the small of her back.

"You got that..." Black Bob nodded and swerved away. They preferred victims who didn't fight back so they abandoned the lick. Some old lady would have to get her purse snatched tonight for their daily bread.

"Is everything ok?" Jennifer asked when the tension registered. She grew up insulated from most dangers so danger was slow to register.

"Better than ok now that I see you again!" he smiled and took her keys. Buddha had seen enough movies to know to open the passenger's side door for her. Once she was seated inside he came around and pulled off.

Jennifer began rambling about teenage stuff while he headed up Ogden avenue. His eyes were pulled over to the gas station that put the thousand dollars in his pocket. It was shut down at the moment since they were running low on product. Plus, it gave the projects and other spots a reprieve so they could sell their own product.

"Huh?" Buddha asked out loud when he saw Joey at the spot. He wanted to dismiss it as coincidence until he saw the unmistakable hand to hand exchange of a dope deal.

"Ju not listening to me!" Jennifer fussed, thinking his 'huh?' was for her.

"Of course! You said Munudo was better than New Edition! I like Force MCs myself," he replied showing his ability to multitask. He had the blessing and curse of being able to focus on more than one thing simultaneously.

Jennifer smiled broadly at being heard, something she didn't get at home. She continued rambling all the way over to City Island. She wanted Sammy's and Buddha intended to deliver, until she found out the swank spot took more than just money. It required reservations and that was the first he heard of it.

They settled for a nice spot with good food. The rich girl exposed him to new foods like lobster and crab legs. Prior to tonight he was chicken wings and whiting fish kind of guy. The starter goatee on his chin even allowed him to order a bottle of wine. It was a night of firsts for the hoodlum from the hood. The fine young thing across the table whet his appetite for the finer things in life. A fair exchange since he wet her appetite in return and dampened her silky panties.

"That was nice!" Jennifer cheered when they got back to her car. She tippy toed up for a kiss when he opened the door for her.

Jennifer practiced kissing with a boy cousin last summer when she visited Puerto Rico but this wasn't like that. This flooded her expensive panties in seconds and had her squirming under his firm clutches. He finally got the chance to grip that fat ass while their tongues twirled.

"Get a room..." someone shouted in passing. The outburst alerted them that they had been making out for several minutes, right there in the parking lot.

"Guess we better go?" Buddha sighed. He hated to break off their make out session and the only place he wanted to go was as deep inside of her as he could.

"Si," she agreed in Spanish and twisted her lips as she sat in the passenger seat. She had seen her mother reaching over to unlock the driver's side her whole life so it came natural.

Jennifer had plenty to say on the way over to City Island but they rode back through the Bronx in silence. Buddha waited for the right time to ask about business and it hadn't come yet.

"We should..." Jennifer blurted as she looked at a neon sign rushing by the window.

"Should what?" Buddha asked and looked around to see what she was looking for. All he saw was a McDonalds and his McDonald's days were over after eating a lobster tail.

"What they said. Get a room. We could..." she explained unsurely. "If you want."

Buddha replied by snatching the wheel so hard the tires squealed as he pulled off the Cross Bronx expressway. A glance in the rearview showed the Holiday day inn sign that made up her mind. The silence they rode in was her determining when, not if to give him some pussy.

"Ju silly!" she cracked up as he dipped in and out of traffic to get her to the hotel.

"Yeah, and you're beautiful!" he replied and made her blush. It was more than just a compliment since he meant every syllable of it. Her good looks were just a part of her beauty. Her laugh and the animated faces she made while she talked added to it.

"For real?" she pleaded. She thought she was but it was worth more coming from a man other than her father.

"Word is bond, the most beautiful girl I ever seen!" he assured with great timing since they just pulled into the hotel parking lot. They walked inside hand in hand like newlyweds.

"ID?" the clerk asked.

"Yeah," Buddha replied and handed over a crisp hundred dollar bill. The clerk nodded at his resemblance of the picture on the bill and handed over a key. The moment of truth came a few moments later when they found themselves face to face in the hotel room.

Buddha took the lead and stuck his tongue back in her

mouth. Their tongues twirled as they removed each other's clothing and fell on the bed. Jennifer moaned and lolled her head as he kissed down her neck. She let out a loud hiss when his lips found her nipples at the same time he touched her juice box.

"Damn!" he grunted at how hot and wet she was when he reached it. They always said Latina's had hot vaginas but this was like a volcano. He grunted again when he tried to put a finger inside and saw how tight it was.

"I'm sorry," she pouted as if she had done something wrong. This was her first time after all so she wasn't sure.

"Don't be," he assured and stuck his tongue back inside of her mouth. He worked his finger tip inside of her until the 'squish' could be heard out loud. That meant it was ready so he reached for his pants to retrieve a rubber. The only protection he found was his pistol. "Shit!"

"What baby?" she purred at the disappointed look on his face. He implemented the 'no glove, no love' policy he lived by. Too many kids in the hood made things harder on themselves by saddling themselves with kids before they were ready.

"Nothing ma," he replied and took position on top of her. They locked eyes as he rubbed the head of his dick on the slippery lips of the inferno between her legs. Her face contorted as he eased inside of her. Her hymen gave way to womanhood when he was halfway in. All that friction, heat and vice like tightness was more than he could stand. More than any man could so he did what any man would and exploded. "Fuck!"

He instantly remembered he was inside of her raw but didn't care. In a way she was his first as well since this was the first time he went raw dog. The exuberance of youth kept his dick hard as a rock and he slowly rocked inside of her.

Jennifer winced from the pain but it was perfectly mixed with pleasure. Exact measures like the saffron and sofrito in her grandmother's arroz con pollo. Soon they kissed vigorously as he slowly stroked her innocence away. After busting inside of her the first time he knew another time wouldn't hurt. So he bust in her a few more times as they made love for a few more hours.

"I'll drive you home," Buddha suggested as they walked hand and hand, man and his woman. Good pussy can affect judgment at times and this was one of those times.

"Please! You wouldn't make it off the block," she said, shaking her head. She was already in trouble, no sense getting him killed as well.

"Well, I'll drive you across the bridge and take a taxi back," he insisted and pressed on. True to his word he crossed the 159th street bridge and pulled over. They were a few blocks from Miguel's dominion so no one saw the exchange.

The cherry red BMW was spotted along fifth and passed along with shouts of 'Oye!' since word was out to be on the lookout for the car. Jennifer arrived home to the busy block all waiting on her. Miguel was relieved she was safe but her mother fussed her out for staying out too late and took her up stairs while Giggles admired her ass.

"**W**ell?" Rip wanted to know the second he opened his door to let Buddha in the apartment.

"Well what?" Buddha shot back in indignation. He assumed he was asking about how his date with Jennifer went. The truth was her pussy felt like a mink laced, heated glove but he wasn't going to tell him that. More like a hot pocket fresh out the microwave but he was keeping that to himself just like her. Because he could still smell her sweet breath in his soul the next morning.

"Well, what she say about the re-up B!" he shot back and matched his energy.

"Oh shit!" he laughed and popped his own forehead. "Damn B! I forgot to even ask."

"That must have been some bomb ass pussy yo!" Rip laughed. He was Puerto Rican himself and knew first hand about that Boricua volcano vagina.

"I'll hit her up now..." he said and headed down the hall to his room. Rip shrugged it off and headed out to the terrace to look over the playground and school that separated their building from the projects. Another good spot to get laid when the weather was nice if you didn't mind an audience. His eyes shot over to the walkway that bridged the gap between University and Ogden avenue.

"Huh?" he asked when he caught the tail end of two people coming out of the park. One was Monte and the other was his mother. That didn't make any sense so he shook it off and looked over Manhattan all the way to Jersey. One day, when his money was right he would move over there. With a back yard, garage, front porch, one day.

"Hola papi!" Jennifer squealed way too loudly when she took Buddha's call. Her vagina was still raw and throbbing from the sex but still gave a tingle when she heard his voice.

"Sup ma. How are you?" he asked out of respect for the virginity she surrendered to him. It was an honor and he was grateful. He was also glad they didn't get around to business and kept it personal.

"Sore!" she giggled and turned her back on Rosalinda who was all in her mouth. She was smart enough to keep this business to herself. He was her Buddha so she was going to keep him to herself.

"My bad," he cheesed and basked in big dick energy. "But look-it, I need to talk business. We have to re-up."

"Well come through. Papi told ju to come back when ju need some more," she reminded. Buddha remembered too, but wanted confirmation before he did.

"Ok, how much does he, they, y'all charge for a kilo?" he asked as his mind flashed to the thirty five Gs Kevin wanted. It was reasonable since he could double that but he still hoped for better.

"Papi charges his people seventeen. Sometimes fifteen," she relayed since she heard her father talking business every day. She expected and waited for a reply but the line was dead air. "Hello. Ju still there?"

"Huh? Oh, yeah. My bad," he said when he caught his breath. The prospect of getting kilos of coke at even seventeen thousand dollars literally took his breath away. It was that exact moment that he realized he was going to be a rich man.

"Just please, don't say my name, or ask about me, or even look in my direction when ju come. Ok?" she warned needlessly. Buddha had already seen the power Miguel Camacho wielded first hand.

"No doubt," he agreed and nodded even though she couldn't see it. He would not be asking or looking for his daughter on his block. Plus, he didn't have to. "When are you coming to see me again?"

"What kind of question is that? Tonight! Quit playing!"

the diva fussed. They said their goodbyes and hung up the phone.

"Who was that!" Rosalinda wanted to know the second the receiver settled in the cradle. Part was her being nosey, the other part was her job.

"Nobody," Jennifer shrugged even though Buddha was everything to her. She felt the same way he did and planned to keep him to herself. After all, the best way to keep a secret is to keep it secret.

CHAPTER 12

"Well?" Rip asked again with a hint of sarcasm since the question at hand should have been asked and answered last night.

"We good B! Better than good!" he cheered as he joined him looking down at the city below and beyond. "Seventeen, maybe even fifteen!"

"So what the fuck Kev talking about, thirty five!" he snarled. He actually felt like the dude tried them with the ridiculous price but Buddha saw through it.

"Son is a small fry! He's gonna be buying from us one day!" Buddha declared. He didn't need a crystal ball to see that far into the near future.

"Word!" his partner nodded although their partnership was about to be tested. "Shit, seventeen is what? Six and a half Gs apiece!"

"Eight and a half but shit, we need to get two more. Three!" he shot back eagerly. Rip twisted his lips ruefully and touched his new medallion dangling from the new chain.

Buddha couldn't read the mind that sent the signals to contort Rip's face so he asked, "What?"

"I'm saying yo! Nawmean," Rip replied almost bashfully.

"Saying what?" he asked since the answer that came to his mind didn't make much sense. Still, he asked, "Yo, I know you ain't blow all your bread B?"

"Huh? Naw, I got plenty bread left! I'm just saying..." he said like it said something when it didn't say shit. "Shit, I'ma put up my sixty five hundred..."

"Eighty five hundred," Buddha corrected again and twisted his lips. Rip could deny all wanted but he knew he fucked his money up.

"Yeah, eight um, t-five. We can just get one and flip it," Rip replied enthusiastically. He may have believed it himself but his friend didn't.

"We can go half on one yo," Buddha agreed and struggled to keep a straight face. He couldn't do it though and his lips twisted on their own. "Get your bread."

"I got it on me!" he shot back and produced a large roll of cash. Buddha squinted at him to see if he was stupid because walking around any part of the Bronx with eight thousand dollars in your pocket was dumb. Doing it in Highbridge was dumb as fuck.

"Oh, ok," Buddha nodded and accepted his promotion. They were called the Buddha crew simply because he was so popular due to his prowess on the basketball court. All that was about to change since he now ran shit. "Let me get your half."

"It's um, seventy eight. I got more at home," Rip admitted and handed off the bread.

"It's cool. I got it," Buddha accepted and added the short money to his. If his friend did anything right it was buying the car since they had too much money to ride the train or bus. Even a gyps cab could be risky if one of the unregulated and unregistered drivers smelled that much cash. They would promptly lock the back doors from the front and kidnap them for it. Either put the money in the slot or burn with the car.

"Here we go..." Buddha said with a sigh when they reached their destination. It could have been in the heart of San Juan Puerto Rico since all the talk, music and aromas were in fluent Spanish.

"We got they attention," Rip advised since he too was fluent in Spanish. He saw Miguel posted up on a 750 BMW so he parked a respectable distance away before opening the doors. Not that they needed to since both sides were snatched open as soon as he pulled into the space.

"Who you looking for B?" a young boricua dared as he looked up at Buddha.

"Him," he replied and nodded up the block at Miguel. He had been so locked in on the man he didn't register the man next to the man until he stood. His tongue instantly ran across the chipped tooth when Giggles stood and marched down the block. Miguel tilted his head curiously to watch whatever this was and was going to be.

"Tranqilo!" Rip fussed when one of the men began to pat him down. Buddha just raised his arms so they could remove the pistol from his waist.

"Sup yo!" Giggles demanded with a murderous mirth twisting the corner of his mouth. It continued twisting into a question mark when he vaguely recognized the faces, just not the places.

"We was here a few weeks back. We did that thing for his family," Buddha said dancing around the murder. Miguel never forgot faces or places and made his way over as well.

"My friends from the Bronx!" he cheered with a smile that didn't quite make it to his eyes.

"Sup yo. You gave us them things and said come back when we needed more?" Buddha reminded a man who never forgot. Nor would he ever forget since he saved his daughter.

"Yes, yes! What took ju guys so long? Business is good in the Bronx," Miguel asked and tilted his head as if it was a casual question. It wasn't and he tuned in explicitly to hear the answer.

"Shit, we the new kids on the block. We ain't wanna bust out and step on toes," Buddha answered honestly. "Shit just go smoother when err body eat. Nawmean?"

"I step on toes! Kick ass and bust heads!" Giggles gushed with a trademark giggle. Rip smiled and nodded along with him since he didn't agree with Buddha's easy approach either. It really didn't matter what either sidekick thought since Miguel's head was still nodding.

"Ju are a smart kid! Once you are established you can dial it up. Bring jour competition to jour side. They will work for ju, not against ju. Understand?" Miguel coached.

"Word," Buddha nodded because he understood perfectly. Common sense is common amongst everyone who possesses it. Both Rip and Giggles didn't and didn't get it. They played checkers, not chess and went head first. Truth be told, either approach can work. One can just go smoother than the others.

"So, how many do ju want?" Miguel asked and answered, 'one,' in his head since one of them was wearing a lot of jewelry. He knew in an instant that they weren't used to money and that could be dangerous. He was worth a couple million dollars but only wore a rubber band on one of his wrist. The Rolex on the other hand and diamond encrusted wedding band were his only indications of wealth.

He wasn't alone since Giggles thought the same number. He had seen Miguel break a few people off a brick or two in exchange for some good deed or another. Only three ever came back for more but only for one. Of them only one came back for another one, one more time before the coke business proved too much for him. Rip nodded mentally since he would have been one of those ones who either fucked off all their money or only managed to hold on to enough to cop one. Buddha wasn't either type.

"Depends on the price?" Buddha asked just as the answer exited the building. He had an advance warning since he heard Jennifer's melodic laughter before she reached the threshold. Plenty of time for him to turn his head in the other direction.

Miguel paid close attention to who looked towards his wife and daughter as they made their way to their car. Most of his workers snapped their heads away but Giggles stole a loving look. Jennifer did the same to Buddha but only Giggles saw her. Only to find his boss looking at him when he looked back. Rip didn't have enough sense not to look either but Miguel expected it.

"Let's go inside and talk business..." Miguel said and turned toward yet another building. He may have figuratively owned the block but he also literally owned a few of the buildings on it.

"I need our bag?" Buddha asked and nodded towards the car. Miguel looked to Giggles who held up the gun he took off him.

"Grab his bag, and give his gun back," the boss said over his shoulder and led the way. There were so many guns in the immediate area he wasn't concerned about them having one. They would both get swiss cheesed before they got off a shot.

They all entered a stark apartment that smelled like cocaine as soon as they stepped inside. It should have considering the hundreds of pounds of the stuff inside. Miguel took a seat on the sofa while everyone else stood. No one spoke until he answered the question asked outside.

"For you, seventeen, five," he decided. He looked to see if the kid would flinch but he didn't and he liked that.

"Let us get three then," he replied and reached for his bag. A nod from Miguel got it relinquished but Buddha could feel the room tense when he went inside. It would have exploded in gunfire had he come up with anything other than the stacks of cash he came out with.

Miguel was both impressed and confused. The kid was definitely a hustler since he turned two into three. What was confusing was the look on his friend's face. They came together but it was clear they were on different pages.

"Word," Rip nodded when the count came up to what it should be. He was already spending the proceeds in his head. Buddha too had some ideas on how to split the proceeds going forward. They both watched when one of the workers returned with their order.

"Ju guys wanna get an extra one?" Miguel tossed out so casually Buddha knew something came with it. If he offered a brick on consignment he knew they were on their way. Once he had their attention he finished the spiel. "Ju know this puta madre they call, Black Bob?"

"Yeah?" they both asked. It was the first time they were unified since they left the Bronx.

"Kill him," Miguel said as plainly as ordering a bagel. It didn't take long to find out who hit their spot on one hundred and sixty fourth street. Now he had to do something about it. Giggles looked like he wanted to cry since he had his black heart set on killing the robbers just like he killed the lieutenant for getting robbed.

"Nah. Bet!" the kids from the Bronx said at the same time. They looked at each other for an explanation. Buddha may have slept like a baby after murdering Black Rob but had no desire to be a hitman for hire. Not even for an extra kilo.

"I'll do it!" Rip said and stuck his chest out. The extra kilo was a hell of an incentive but he also wanted to bust his gun. He loved Buddha like a brother but didn't like him beating him in everything. That's why he tacitly competed with him in everything. Which was why he spent so much money to outshine his partner.

Buddha turned and looked at his friend while Miguel looked at him. This too was a test of his leadership. If he checked his friend in front of them he wouldn't be a good one. Sometimes a leader has to follow and Buddha was a leader. He pulled the bag open to accommodate the extra brick.

CHAPTER 13

Best friends are somewhat like married couples. They learn and accept each other's strong points and let them lead. This is why Rip handled the measuring while Buddha handled the cooking. The Buddha crew anxiously awaited them to finish so they could hit the block. Their concentration killed all conversation until Rip spoke what was on his mind.

"We gonna have to kill both them niggas..." Rip concluded. Once again it was a few seconds behind since Buddha already knew that. Killing Black Bob meant Tone-Capone had to go as well enough if his name wasn't mentioned.

"A-yo, go grab us some White Owls," Buddha told Trouble. They both looked at the fresh box of cigars on the table but neither acknowledged them.

"Bet," the kid said and rushed out to fill the request. He was so happy to finally keep money in his pocket he didn't ask for more to make the needless purchase. Anytime

Buddha sent him for food, beer or whatever, he gladly used his own money.

"Word," Buddha agreed once they were alone. It wasn't that he didn't trust young Trouble but still wasn't going to talk about murders in front of him. Or anyone who didn't need to know. "Gonna have to whack both them niggas."

"How you think we should get 'em?" Rip asked. He tried to make it sound casual but had no idea. It wasn't as simple as just going up into the projects and gunning them down. The kitchen went silent as he contemplated how to kill the two killers. Killing either at any time wouldn't be easy. Killing them both, at the same time would be a bitch.

"A bitch! Them niggas like tricking off with bitches. We need a bitch to trick them back..." he concluded.

"That nigga Tone be tryna spit at Yvonne. Shit, we can use her for bait," Rip snarled. Buddha knew where he was going with it and thought it through.

"This is a murder bruh..." he reminded. Even Black Bob and Tone-Capone used chicks to set up victims to be robbed but this was murder and they didn't need any witnesses. He entertained the idea in his mind until it led to the vision of having to kill her too so she could never talk about it. Mia certainly gossipped about everything she saw and heard anytime he went over there. He would go for ass and leave with tea. "Nah B."

"Well, we gotta do something. We already got paid," he reminded. Buddha let out a deep sigh since Rip was the one who took the payment and hit. Now he had to make sure it got done. The doorbell rang before Trouble walked back inside with Monte and E-baby.

"I smell money!" E-baby cheered when he smelled the freshly cooked coke. He saw both men wearing bandanas on their faces but didn't register. He was ready to get some work so he could get some money.

"Y'all can help bag it up!" Rip ordered and pointed to the piles of crack and empty vials on the dining room table. The four minus Rip stood around to cut the crack and fill the vials. He posted up on the terrace and looked down over his domain.

A smirk turned his mouth up into murderous mirth when he saw their intended targets escorting a crack head over to Nelson park. The children used the steel castle as a fort during the day but it was a great place to get your dick sucked at night.

Black Bob and Tone-Capone liked to trick off together just like they robbed and plundered together. It was only right that they die together. He now had the where, it was just a matter of when and exactly how. It wouldn't be tonight since he had other plans. He planned to bust something alright, but it wouldn't be his gun.

"Y'all can hit the block now," Rip ordered since he wanted to give orders. It was the same order Buddha would have given since they needed to recoup what they just spent. Monte and E-baby got a 'G-pack' each which meant they had to bring back seven hundred and fifty dollars. The rest was theirs since they got a raise, and that's not a bad day's work for just a few hours.

"A-yo, let me spit at you before you go?" Buddha asked. He was careful not to order Rip in front of the workers.

"Sup B?" he asked as the last of the workers filed out.

"I just been thinking about the pay scale," he offered, paused, then continued. "We can't be looking crazy when it's time to re-up. From now on, let's split twenty five off the hundred too and flip the rest?"

"So..." Rip began and drew a blank since math wasn't his strong point. His face morphed into a mask of confusion as he tried to figure it out. Buddha was slightly amused but didn't have time to bask in it.

"So if we do a buck, twenty five Gs goes to the workers. We split another twenty Gs, and flip the fifty," he spelled out. That too was followed by a moment of silence as Rip tried to see if it was enough to floss with. He had twenty five grand hanging off his neck right now.

"So..." he asked and twisted his lips to help think.

"So, if we run through this work in a week or two we'll be seeing twenty or thirty Gs. A week," he said and sealed the deal. That nodded his friend's head in agreement. "You going down?"

"For a minute. Gotta lay this pipe!" Rip said and gripped his dick through his pants.

"Check," he agreed and began to clean up the mess made from cooking a whole kilo of coke. They only packaged a few ounces so the rest was left in the bags and tucked away. Just in time before his mother walked in.

"Ung! What's that smell?" Denise reeled and scrunched her face. She saw Rip was present and had an idea. "You over her cooking some of that Spanish food?"

"No miss Denise," he laughed and shook his head. The food they just cooked was for Spanish, black, blue or yellow as long as they produced that green. "See you later, Miss Denise."

"Tell your moms I said hello," she called after him as he left. Rip grunted in reply since he had no idea when he would see the woman next. Monte was seeing her at the moment, bobbing her head as she slobbed on his knob. Buddha lit frankincense to kill the smell.

"What are you about to do?" Buddha asked. He tried to sound casual and would have to anyone else except the woman who raised him thus far.

"No, a better question is, what do you think, you are about to do?" she shot back and laughed. "And don't say nothing, cuz you don't be cleaning up for nothing! Lighting incense for nothing..."

"I'm saying tho," he said almost bashfully.

"I got to meet this one!" his mother laughed and sat on the sofa. She leaned back and crossed her legs like she wasn't going anywhere.

"Ma! Look, here's two hundred bucks. Catch a taxi to the Deuce. Eat, see a movie..." he said and came out with a bribe.

"Weed too!" she insisted after tucking the money away. Buddha sighed, twisted his lips and dug into his pocket to part with his personal weed. She accepted it but didn't budge. "And I still wanna meet her!"

"You be 'buggin ma," he pouted but knew it was all he could do. It was her house after all so she made the rules. Time had gotten away from him so he rushed out and down stairs to meet Jennifer before any of the local jackers did. Black Bob and Tone-Capone may have been the most notorious but they weren't the only stickup kids in Highbridge by a long shot.

The timing was good since a rare parking spot opened in front of the building just as Jennifer crossed over 166th. Buddha blocked it with his body and waved her over. He called some of the younger kids from the building over since they had to stay in front of the building. They were free to roam from one end of the block to the next but that still provided plenty to see and do.

"Y'all wanna make twenty bucks?" he offered and dug into

his pocket. It was purely rhetorical in his mind since who doesn't wanna make twenty bucks. Even if a billionaire was asked he'll probably ask what he has to do.

"A-yo B, it's four of us! That's just five bucks each!" one of the little girls fussed and rolled her neck.

"We need ten bucks, each," her brother nodded. Jennifer smiled brightly as her boyfriend negotiated with the kids.

"Seven bucks each and y'all gotta make sure no one gets too close," he countered. "No sitting on it, no smudges."

"Eight and you got a deal!" the girl said and extended her small hand to seal the deal. Buddha had been buying the kids ice cream all summer so they had to try him up.

"A'ight ma. You got that," he sighed and shook her hand. He came out of his pocket with a twenty and handed it over. "Half now, the other half when we come out."

"Ju are so sweet!" Jennifer pouted as if she might cry. She wrapped her arm in his as they headed inside. They almost made it before Yvonne and Lisa stepped outside.

"Un-uh! That don't look like no Mia!" Lisa fussed to Yvonne who quickly cosigned. She probably wouldn't have said anything if she had been alone but she wasn't so she pressed up.

"Sure don't," she snarled and looked Jennifer up and down. The snarled deepened when she realized all the brands lacing Jennifer's body were as official as a ref's whistle. Still, she was loyal to her girl who was dealing with Buddha. "Um, sup with this?"

"This, is my girl," he shrugged and continued inside. The hood rats were supposed to be on the way to the bodega but spun the block to the projects to get their girl. Jennifer's arm tightened around his at being called his girl since he was definitely her man.

They had to share the elevator to the eighth floor where the rider got off. The door hadn't closed all the way before she shoved her tongue into his mouth. Neither could get enough of the other and they practically devoured each other until the door dinged and opened on the sixteenth floor. He led her down the hall and inside.

"Oh my gosh! She's so pretty!" Denise gushed at her son's girlfriend. He had others but none made him bashful like she witnessed earlier. That's why she had to meet her.

"Thank ju!" she gushed and blushed under her brown skin. The accent came through and told his mother she was Puerto Rican.

"Ma, this is Jennifer. Jennifer, ma," he introduced but didn't close the door behind them in hopes she would be leaving.

"Hello miss Jackson," she greeted even though she wanted to call her ma as in mother in law one day. Buddha blew his breath in exasperation since he wanted to be alone.

"I can take a hint B!" Denise laughed and stood. She checked the girl over as she exited the apartment. She intended to take him up on the exact offer and enjoy dinner and a movie. She shot her son a thumbs up of approval behind Jennifer's back as she left.

"She likes you," he confirmed once he closed and locked the door behind them. His mother was one of those people whose mind could be clearly read by the look on her face. She couldn't hide if she was happy, angry or sad if she wanted to.

"Oh my God! Yes!" Jennifer cheered and spun. Her father would never accept Buddha and probably kill him before he accepted him but it felt good to be liked. It felt even better to be touched so she touched him.

"You better be careful with that..." he warned when she got a firm grip on his dick through his jeans.

"Nope!" she said and moved in for a kiss. The kiss carried them down the hall and into his room. They only paused long enough to come out of their clothes and meet on the bed. The twin size wasn't wide enough to have a middle but it wasn't needed since he slid in the middle of her legs.

The feverous kisses took him all over her thick lips, neck and breast. He sucked her hard nipples and fondled her juice box making her writhe and moan. Her hard stomach begged to be kissed so he kissed down and around to her navel.

"Eat me!" Jennifer pleaded so urgently Buddha found himself face to face with some pussy. Rosalinda had always bragged about dudes eating her box and had her curious. Meanwhile, Mr 'I don't, won't ever eat no pussy, period' had a dilemma on his hands and the prettiest pussy on the planet right in his face. He had seen a few vaginas in his life but never from this close and never quite this pretty.

All that shit went out the window when he leaned in and took a lick. The flick of his tongue got a loud hiss that lifted Jennifer's body off the mattress. He was sold on eating pussy just like the roar of an engine sells a sports car. Eating pussy doesn't come with instructions but then again, it really doesn't need any. He let her moves and moans be his guide and sucked that young box until she literally screamed.

"I'm coming!" Jennifer declared and kept her word as the first orgasm of her life wracked her whole body. Likewise, he was sold on eating pussy just from pleasing his girl. Any man not interested in pleasing his woman is just weird.

Jennifer snatched him up to her face and sucked her own juices off his lips and face. It took a second, because it was a lot of juice. So much juice his dick slipped inside of her slippery lips. She was still so tight he had to push to get inside. So he pushed inside and began to stroke.

All she could do was grimace and grip the sheets as he took her to 'pound-town'. Buddha was determined not to go out bad and bust quick nuts like the last time. Nope, this time he dug her young ass out real good. He bottomed out in her box when the tingles shot through his body. His eyes shot to the condoms on the dresser as he bust a nut inside of her.

"Fuck!" he announced for that reason, plus she felt good as fuck. So good he stayed put and fucked her again.

CHAPTER 14

"I have to go," Jennifer pouted when she looked at the clock. She was on the verge of tears since she wanted to stay. Buddha let out a sigh but he felt like crying himself.

"Yeah," he agreed so she wouldn't get in trouble. Nor did he want his mother to return and catch them laid up. He decided then he needed his own spot then twisted his lips at the thought of leaving his mother. His head shook at the thought since he wasn't leaving her here by herself.

"Ju ok?" she asked of the conflicted look on his face.

"Huh? Oh, yeah. I'm cool!" he assured and confirmed with a smile and kiss on her mouth. They dressed and headed down the hall to the elevator and moped the whole way down. Their fingers intertwined as they made their way through the lobby. Buddha looked out the large windows and saw trouble. "Fuck!"

"What's wrong baby?" she pleaded like whatever bothered him was a bother to her as well. She got the answer for herself when Mia banged on the glass.

"Yeah, bring your ass out here!" Mia demanded and smeared more vaseline on her face.

"Jour ex I take?" Jennifer laughed and picked up her face. She was a sheltered, rich girl but was definitely with the shits. She was a Camacho after all and they didn't back down for anyone. Plus her father had her in karate, judo and jujitsu since she was five years old.

"Not even?" he had to ask since he never claimed the girl or gave her a title. He did fuck her a few times a week so she was whatever that made her.

"Ju got a problem?" Jennifer wanted to know when she stepped outside. Buddha tried to get in between but she was the aggressor.

"Yeah bitch. I fight about my man!" Mia declared and put up her hands.

"Except, I'm not your man so you already lost that battle," Buddha corrected and turned to Rip standing by with a silly grin. A silly grin that confused Buddha since his partner knew who this girl was and what was at stake. Not just losing the connect but their lives as well. Miguel Camacho and Giggles would air this shit out about his daughter. He knew Yvonne and Lisa would jump in once it popped off. "Get them!"

"Oh yeah," he laughed and grabbed the extras. It was a fair fight now but Buddha didn't want to take any chances.

"Go home Mia," Buddha demanded.

"Nigga you not my man! You can't tell me what to do!" she shot back. She evidently missed the contradiction and rushed at Jennifer.

'Hi-yah!' the girl shouted and beat Mia up in the blink of an eye. The girl kicked her in her stomach and met her with an uppercut when she doubled over. It stood her back up right in the path of a three piece combo that rang her bell.

"Yooooo!" Rip laughed as Mia's friends pulled away from him. They didn't want any of what she just got so they bent over to help her up. Buddha continued to walk his girl to her car so she could get home.

"Let me take a look..." Buddha challenged the car watchers when they arrived. They weren't worried since it was just like they left it a couple hours ago.

"Un-huh! Pay up!" the little spokesperson demanded. Buddha nodded and gave them another twenty to share between them. The remains of chips, drinks and candy on the ground was from the last twenty they already spent.

"Good job," he said and looked down the block to where his other workers were making real money. E-baby and Monte had sold out and been replaced by Big Hank and Joey. Jennifer met him with her lips when he turned back to face her.

"Oooh!" the little girl giggled and cooed before taking off for the bodega with her friends. It gave them the break they needed or they would have made out, right there for another hour.

"Call me when you get home," he demanded.

"Si papi," she agreed with a pout that almost made his dick hard again. She pulled away as Yvonne and Mia helped their wobbly friend away from the building.

"I'ma tell my brother what you did!" Mia fussed over her shoulder as they headed for the projects.

"You gonna get your brother knocked off," Rip said to her wake as it faded into black on the walkway between the building. He was still waiting to bust his cherry by busting his gun. He hadn't got to their intended targets just yet but anyone could get it.

"Kev ain't crazy," Buddha laughed. Kev had ears so he knew what his sister was about. A drama queen who fucked a lot of dudes and smoked woolie blunts. Plus he wanted to put Buddha on his team, while Buddha was thinking the same. Once he got his weight up Kev and his crew would be selling for him.

"Yoooo! I just waxed both they assess! Yvonne and Lisa!" he cheered like fucking them both was a prize. Both were smoking woolie blunts on a regular basis so they had lots of threesomes, foursome and other freaky shit in their future. Once they moved up and got that glass dick in their mouth the sky was the limit on what they would do.

"Might as well make it a threesome next time and hit Mia too. I'm done with her ass," he said as they headed over to their spot. They oversaw the operations until the next Gpacks were done. All while plotting on a murder, or two.

※

"Y'all tryna get sucked off or nah?" Tonya asked. It was more like a dare since she didn't wait for an answer before walking off. Black Bob and his crime partner were smoking the last of their weed. They bought it with the last of the money they stole from Alejandro's stash house.

They lived for the moment so it was only fitting for them to fuck off the money as fast as humanly possible. They both had the new Bally sneakers, Coogi sweaters and Calvin Klein jeans. Both loaded their closets before blowing ten grand apiece on the large hollow chains with chunky, diamond studded medallions.

"Bitch ain't even ask if we had dough?" Tone-Capone wondered as he locked on her round ass shifting away from them towards the park.

"Shit, you must want to donate a blow job to our cause," Black Bob shrugged and stood. He fell instep behind Tonya and led the way to lead the train they planned to run on her tonsils.

"I should fuck this bitch?" Tone asked since he accepted his position as a side kick.

"Word," his leader agreed since the clock was ticking before there wasn't much left to fuck. Tonya had started smoking woolies a few months ago before getting a stripe and graduating to the pipe. It wouldn't be long until she looked like the bobblehead veteran crack heads.

"Ugh!" a loud grunt echoed in the darkness of Nelson park at night. It emanated from the fort which meant it was occupied but from the sound of it, was about to be vacant. Monte hopped down from the fort and helped Alva down. They headed out one exit while the next residents entered from the other direction.

"I'm trying to fuck," Tone-Capone announced once they ascended up into the club house.

"Me first!" Bob shot back and whipped out the dick. He probably should have pulled his gun out instead. A loud 'click' in the darkness froze everyone in place. They all looked in different directions until they came face to face with the barrel of a gun.

"Nah, him first..." the face behind the gun barrel announced just before he shot Tone-Capone in his face.

"The fuck B! We ain't got no beef with y'all Rip!" Black Bob pleaded and raised his hands. They were indeed scheming on hitting their spot but hadn't made a move. So technically no beef, not yet.

"Yeah you do. You hit our people on 164. Nowwe hitting back," Rip explained and took aim. "Oh yeah, before you go, My boy Buddha killed yo bitch ass brother. You mine tho..."

A tug on the trigger made the gun bark and spark in the crisp night air. Black Bob tried to make a move but the bullet caught him in his face and flipped him out of the iron fort. Rip aimed down and fired a few more rounds at him on the ground.

"We good?" Tonya asked since she had done her part by luring the men here. She had done it a few times for the dead men but Rip outbid them.

"Yeah, we good," he said and looked down at what was left of Tone-Capone. Then, turned to leave.

"Can I get a few more caps?" she asked before he could get away.

"Huh?" he asked with a pained expression since she had been paid well for her part. A vital part so he softened, sighed and went into his pocket. "Ion walk around with jums, so here..."

"Thank you," she said politely and accepted the extra hundred dollars. They both hopped down from the crime scene and headed in different directions.

✥

Dead mufuckas had never been a priority in the Bronx simply because they were dead mufuckas. What's the rush. That's why it was nearly afternoon when the first police arrived in Nelson park. It wasn't until an old lady

WE RUN NEW YORK

walked over to the precinct and demanded, 'y'all come get this dead mufucka out the damn park'.

"This mufucka is dead," one cop assured the other as he looked at the body in the fort.

"Looks like someone else got hit too?" the other said from ground level as he looked at the blood congealing on the asphalt. "Let's call homicide."

"Fuck going on?" Buddha asked as Rip happily led him to the park. The growing crowd of gawkers and official vehicles said something happened.

"I took care of that business is what happened," Rip announced and simultaneously stuck out his chest and lifted his chin. Even Yvonne benefitted from the morale boost the murder gave him. Rip was so charged up from the shooting he went over there last night and fucked the daylights out of her until daylight.

"Bob?" he asked as they tried to squeeze through the crowd.

"And bitch ass Tone-Capone," he nodded. Except there was one problem.

"I just see one body?" Buddha asked and scanned the park again. Tone could clearly be seen but Black Bob was nowhere to be found. He managed to survive the shooting and make it all the way out to Coney Island and into the emergency room. It was a straight shot on the D train but all those holes in him made it seem a lot longer. Only in New York does a man leaking from several bullet holes get ignored on the subway.

"Yo I shot both them niggas B!" Rip swore and turned heads. He turned his own head and saw Buddha making haste out of the park. He laughed off the outburst and tried to clean it up. "On the video game. Shot all them asteroids!"

"Why is he naked tho?" a detective asked since Tone's corpse had been stripped down to the bone. The neighborhood crack heads had been picking on the body like vultures. The first ones searched his pockets but came up empty. They settled for his chains and rings to trade for drugs. The next went through his pockets before taking his shoes and jeans. The Coogi sweater was soaked in blood but could be and would be washed out and sold too. Soon nothing remained but a dead mufucka with a hole in his face. Luckily there was no market for bullets or someone would have dug it out and sold it as well.

"Fuck!" Rip fussed when he finally accepted that Black Bob had not only survived but had gotten away. He spun on his heels and marched back over to Ogden ave. He headed up the block and found his crew at the spot. Buddha was sitting on a car pouting and smoking a blunt.

"Let me talk to my man B," Buddha told Trouble when he saw Rip coming over. The kid hopped up quickly since he was always eager to comply. "The fuck son?"

"Yo B, word to my moms I blasted that nigga in his face! He flipped over the fort and I pumped like, four more slugs into the nigga!" Rip vowed. He did indeed shoot Bob in his face but it tore through one side of his cheek and out the other. Painful and disfiguring but far from fatal. All four shots he fired bounced harmlessly off the asphalt and missed.

"He ain't dead tho," was his reply. He pondered over what that meant with Miguel but another thought interceded. "Now he's gonna be gunning for you."

'Gunning for us' Rip thought and twisted his lips. His little revelation about what happened to Black Rob came back to mind and put a target on his friend's back as well.

"Well, we can tell Miguel I got them niggas. One dead, the

other ain't coming back around here no more!" Rip declared victoriously. They paused the conversation when Monte started in their direction. He was part of the crew but wasn't down with the murder so it wouldn't be discussed in his presence.

"Yo! They say Tone-Capone got bodied in Nelson park!" he gossiped and proved them right. Buddha already knew he really wasn't about this life and was way to happy to be reporting a murder.

"Word?" They both asked as if they both hadn't just left the crime scene.

"Word! I was out there just before it happened! Heard the shots and err thing!" the kid cheered.

Rip twisted his lips dubiously since he didn't see him in the park. He did see his own mother leaving the fort before the victims arrived but that didn't go together at all and was promptly dismissed.

"Word," Rip chuckled. The laughter was cut short when he saw Joey heading into the bodega across the street. He recognized the bling bouncing on his chest and called him over. "A-yo Joey! Come here!"

"Peace, peace," Joey huffed, slightly winded from rushing across the street and nearly being run down by the bus.

"Where the fuck you get this from!" Rip barked and lifted the medallion from his chest. It was the same one the late Tone-Capone rocked when he was alive.

"You like that huh!" he bragged and nodded. "Some crack let me get it for ten vials last night!"

"Word?" Buddha asked since that was a good deal. He certainly would have bought it but had to wonder how when they sold out and closed up shop long before the ambush in the park. Nothing was making sense but it was about to get worse. Way worse when Tonya ambled on the scene.

"Yo Rip, let me get a few," she semi demanded.

"You better push up on one of them!" Buddha snapped and pointed with his head towards the workers. He and Rip just supervised and didn't make sales anymore.

"I ain't got no money. Hook me up?" she insisted.

"As much as I hit you with last night! The fuck you do with all that!" Rip fussed.

"Bruh, I'ma crackhead! The fuck you think I did! Smoked that shit!" she shot back. Rip sighed and dug into his pocket. He counted off a hundred and handed it off.

"Here, but that's it! Don't keep coming back err five damn minutes!" he growled. Buddha watched as she took the money over to Hank and cop some vials.

"Yeah, that nigga probably bled to death somewhere," Rip decided but Buddha hadn't moved beyond what just happened. Rip didn't give anyone anything for nothing so he had to wonder.

"The fuck was that B?" he asked. He had a sinking feeling in his soul when he heard the answer.

"Man, I used that bitch to get Black Bob and Tone to the park. Shot her a hundred bucks!" he explained casually while Buddha was nearly losing his mind. "Now she comes back for more!"

"She's going to keep coming back for more! For the rest of her life son! The fuck son!" Buddha reeled. It was bad but he needed to know just how bad. "You murked the nigga in front of her?"

"Yeah, I..." Rip was saying but Buddha got up and walked off again shaking his head. Trouble was looking at him and gave him something to fuss about. "The fuck you looking at!"

CHAPTER 15

"Here we fucking go," Buddha sighed when he spotted Kev as soon as he entered the project's court yard. This could go a few different ways but the gun in his waist could too. He tried to gauge his mood by the look on his face but it was blank. He would find out since he was now on the scene. "Sup B?"

"You my nigga," he replied and stood to dap him up. That was a good sign but it got better when he cracked a smile. "You heard about Bob and Tone?"

"Yeah..." Buddha replied and managed to remain neutral since he was connected to the killings. Kev caught the stoicism and explained.

"Yo son, I'm not bugging over you and my sister. That's y'all shit B. She said you held her down while your new girl hit her. Lisa told me it was a head up," he advised as they stepped out of earshot from the rest of his workers.

"Word," Buddha replied and muted himself. Sometimes it's best to be quiet and let other people show their hand. The more quiet, the more they reveal.

"So, what y'all niggas decide? Y'all tryna get down with the get down!" Kev cheered like it was the best thing since American cheese on a Jamaican beef patty. Which is pretty damn good but Buddha still had to decline. Stall actually, to delay the inevitable fall out that was sure to come.

"They thinking about it. It's just we got fronted some work from Alejandro on one six four..." he decided. It was a gamble to name drop but the name recognition flashed in the man's irises. Word on the street was that Tone Capone got whacked after he and Black Bob hit their spot. Tone got splatted while Black Bob hadn't been seen or heard from since. No one mourned the two stickup kids except maybe their mothers, maybe.

"Word, word," Kev nodded in disappointment.

"Now, if you can match what they doing then hell yeah!" Buddha said and put the weight back on him. Kev knew he wasn't dealing with that kind of weight just yet and shook his head. He knew he had him where he wanted him so he drove it home. "We rather be with you anyway, big bruh."

"Word up B!" Kev nodded in agreement. "Just stay down until I come up. Word is bond I'm about to run Highbridge!"

"Word!" Buddha cheered like he bought into what he was selling. The crew on the bench watched the two men dap and hug in relief. This could have gone another way and they liked Buddha too much to have to kill him. They would have, they just wouldn't like it. They were the only ones who liked seeing the two men making peace.

"Un-uh! That nigga let his girl jump me and you hugging the nigga! You soft as baby shit B!" Mia shouted from the window. The shiny black eye Jennifer gave her was visible from the ground.

"Go back in the window!" Kev shouted up.

"Tuh!" Mia huffed and fell back onto the sofa. She was mad at both Buddha and her brother and planned to get them both back. She wasn't sure how just yet, but someday, somehow they would get theirs. In the meanwhile she marched down the hall and into her brother's bedroom.

She knew exactly where he hid his stash so she went straight for it. Ignoring the stacks of cash since he kept her purse and pockets filled with cash. She was in search of one thing he wouldn't give her. She could have found the coke with her eyes closed since the smell was so strong.

"Thank you," she hissed as she grabbed a handful of his blue capped vials. She wanted to roll up a nice fat woolie blunt to blast her emotions to the moon but their mutual mother was home. A chance glance out the window showed Tonya coming into the building. She lived a flight up so Mia headed out the apartment, up the stairs and met her by her door.

"Sup?" Tonya asked since she didn't hang out with the girl. She was only a few years older but that meant more in high school.

"Huh? Nah, I'm tryna smoke but my moms is home," she explained.

"Say word," Tonya agreed and pulled her keys. She knew what that was like once upon a time. Now that welfare was paying her own rent she didn't have that problem anymore.

"Where the kids?" Mia asked when she saw scattered toys but no kids to play with them.

"With my baby father," she said with relief when the relief went to him for getting his kids away from the crackhead.

"Shit!" Mia fussed when she realized she forgot her weed and cigars in her haste to catch her. "You got weed? I'm tryna roll me up a woolie!"

"Girl them things a waste of time and good drugs!" she said and whipped out her pipe like a King's guard pulls his sword. The jury was still out on which one was more dangerous. "You tryna get high or nah?"

"I ain't never..." Mia was saying as she watched the woman chip a piece off the old rock and load it on the tip of the straight shooter.

Tonya seemed to go into a trance when the long orange flame emerged from a flick of her Bic. A loud sizzle filled the space between the heaven and earth when the flame touched the drug. Her eyes went as wide as dinner plates when she sucked the stream of smoke from the rock into her soul.

The tip of the pipe still smoked when Tonya fell back onto her sofa. She took in sips of air as if trying to keep the smoke inside her lungs. She held her breath long enough to make Aqua man say 'damn', then blew out a plume of noxious gray smoke towards the ceiling.

"Hmp!" Tonya huffed as she passed the pipe with such urgency Mia felt inclined to take it. She followed suit and inhaled what was left of the rock on the pipe. Even she knew her life had changed by the time she exhaled.

There was no special ceremony commemorating the event but she just received her stripes and graduated to the pipe. They spent the rest of the day smoking the stash Mia had swiped from her brother.

"Girl fire that shit up!" Tonya urged when Mia tried to slow down when they neared the end of her supply. "Don't worry, I get this shit for free!"

"Oye," Giggles said when he spotted Rip's whip pulling up the block after clearing security on the corner. No one could just pull onto the block without being cleared. Ironically the block full of killers was probably the safest place in the city.

"I've been expecting them," Miguel nodded. Buddha had checked in with his lieutenant Jorge after the hit and was summoned.

"What we gonna tell them?" Rip wondered since the job was only half done.

"The truth," Buddha said and patted the bag on his lap. His pistol was under the seat but that's where it would stay. He took the lead once they stepped from the car and headed to where the boss was seated.

"Mi amigos from the Bronx!" Miguel cheered and stood to shake their hands.

"Uh, sup yo," Buddha replied skeptically. The man seemed happy to see them and that didn't make sense since they weren't friends. They weren't foes either so he shook the outstretched hand.

"I heard ju guys took care of that business for me!" the man cheered. His eyes narrowed from the wide smile but he was still watching closely for their reactions. Buddha noticed the smile didn't line up with the lines in his brow but Rip missed it and beamed proudly.

"Yeah, I did that!" Rip announced and ran with it. "I blasted both those puta madres!"

"Word?" Giggles asked but got shut down by a glance from the boss. He too knew it's better to be quiet and listen.

"One survived. Black Bob," Buddha was quick to add. Not that Miguel didn't already know that since he had a whole crew in Highbridge. He knew that too so he presented the bag.

"He ain't been seen since. But if he do..." Rip added while Giggles intercepted the bag and pulled it open. He squinted curiously at the content before turning it over to the boss.

"What is this?" Miguel asked even though he knew American dollars better than most Americans. He had millions of them in one of the apartments upstairs. And dope worth millions more in another. Still, the question was rhetorical since he was pretty sure what it was for.

"Seventeen for the other key. We didn't complete the job," he said and stuck his chest out. Thug or no thug Buddha had honor. A rare trait in his chosen profession, but one sorely needed.

"Ju will tho," Miguel said and handed it back before turning to his own crew. "Ju see this guy! I like his style!"

The men all smiled and dapped Buddha up except a few. Two actually since Rip didn't like being shown up any more than Giggles did. He glared at Buddha so intently he was the only one who saw when his eyes glanced upward. He would have thought nothing about it if they didn't sparkle. Giggles followed his gaze upward and saw the same sparkle in Jennifer's eyes. She saw him watching and ducked back inside.

"We're going shopping," Esmeralda announced as she came through the living room. Jennifer and Rosalinda were close behind for the trip so Giggles immediately stood to drive and protect them.

"I got them," Miguel decided and stood to spend the day

with his ladies. Both Rosalinda and Giggles fell back to let the family enjoy family time. There was no need for additional security since Miguel was as dangerous as anyone. Plus, there wasn't much danger in Saks fifth avenue or Tavern on the Green.

They sat back down and looked at whatever was on the TV for a few minutes after being left alone. Once they were sure no one was doubling back for something left behind they made their move. Giggles let out a giggle as he kicked his sneakers off and stood to remove his jeans. Rosalinda just leaned back and shimmied out of her Liz Claiborne jeans before pulling off her shirt. She left her bra and panties on since part of the fun of getting a gift is in unwrapping it.

He left nothing to unwrap except for his socks. Meanwhile a thick erection stood out between them. He playfully bopped her on her head with it before she ate it up. Giggles giggled while she gobbled the dick. He unhooked her bra and fondled her nipples until they were as hard as his dick. She leaned back so he could remove her panties and play in her pussy while she topped him off.

"Fuck!" he shouted and pulled out of her mouth before it got the best of him. The mouth was superb but the pussy was even better. Juicy and loose enough to really pound. Miguel would fuck her slow and easy when he fucked her but Giggles was the opposite. He took a few introductory strokes at different angles before lifting her thick legs onto his shoulders. She let out a sigh at what she knew was coming.

Giggles got his footing and commenced to take her to pound town. The sounds of squishy pussy and skin slapping soon echoed around the otherwise quiet apartment. She managed to bust a nut during the nearly violent pounding.

The contractions and gush of juice pushed him over the edge as well.

"Open your mouth..." he directed and she complied by opening his mouth as he snatched from her snatch. He stuffed himself back in her mouth just in the nic of time and bust directly on her tonsils. She clamped down and took it all down her throat. Hisknees buckled from the sensation but whose wouldn't. Rosalinda smiled as much as a girl can smile with a dick in her mouth. Not only did she enjoy pleasing her suitors in this way but swallowing also doubled as birth control.

"Mmmmm," she purred when he fell onto the sofa, spent from the intense nut. He wished it was Jennifer on the receiving end but this was the next best thing. He watched her large ass jiggle down the hall as she went to retrieve a washcloth to wash them up.

"Sup with Jennifer and that black kid?" Giggles asked as she washed her own juices off his balls and thighs. He knew what he saw the last time Buddha was on the block but not what it meant. If anyone would know it was her. Which was why she was on his payroll as well. He fed her dick and dollars to keep him informed on both Jennifer and her father.

"From the Bronx?" she asked immediately. That was the only black kid she knew of so she didn't wait for him to reply. "I know she liked him. Don't know if she sees him?"

"Hmp?" he huffed. It wasn't much since Jennifer knew enough not to let her know anything. "Keep an eye out and let me know."

"Ok papi," she agreed. All that washing with the warm wash cloth made Giggles grow hard and long in her hand once again.

"Bente," he said and pulled her onto his lap. She wriggled him inside of her and bounced until he started making faces again. She waited until he howled before hopping off, dropping down and adding brunch to the lunch she swallowed already.

CHAPTER 16

Trouble now spent most of his days over in Highbridge. Lately he had begun spending most of his nights there as well. He would camp out on E-baby's sofa after E-baby caught him sleeping in the stairwell. He still ventured over to Jerome ave to check on the grandmother who raised him as much as she could. It felt nice to bring her some money or food. His old partner was usually on a lick or on the run from a lick so they rarely crossed paths, until today.

"Word B?" Manny cheered when he saw Trouble walking up to their building. Something he did less of the more he spent time over in Highbridge. He enviously eyed his new sneakers, clothes and fresh haircut. Buddha kept him fresh since he started working for him. In the few months not only had he put on a few pounds but grew an inch or two. Good nutrition has that effect on a growing boy.

"I told you yo," Trouble reminded. He tried to convince his crime partner into coming with him but he refused. The raggedy Adidas and holey jeans spoke to the wisdom and outcome of that choice. Life is nothing but a series of choices and he was making bad ones.

Manny preferred to get his the easy way and stick a gun in people's faces. So far no one wanted their stuff more than their life. Even he knew it would eventually catch up with him. There are only two ends for stickup kids, a holding cell in jail or a holding drawer at the morgue. He stuck to soft targets like old people and small kids with grocery lists. Especially after the last lick on Fordham nearly got them killed. It got Trouble a job but he was still out here in the streets. The kid tried selling for one of the local dope boys but just ran off with the pack. Some people just can't do right, he was some people.

"Can you put me on?" Manny heard himself ask. Only because he had to say it loud enough to be heard over the grumble of his empty stomach.

"Ion know. I'll spit at Buddha and see," he admitted since he was just a look out. Even so it allowed him to get fresh and keep money in his pockets. "Run and grab us some wings while I check on G-ma dukes."

"Word," Manny agreed and eagerly accepted the twenty dollar bill he extended. His first nature told him to take the money and run. Again, some people are just no good and Manny was one of them. He had stolen everything he could for as long as he could at home until his mother put him out. His grandmother took him in and he cleaned her out as well. It was only the knot he saw on his old friend's pocket that kept him honest. Only because there was more from where this twenty came from. He would stay down and try to come up.

Trouble returned from blessing his grandmother with a few hundred as well as his presence. She was delighted to see him changing for the better even if it was from selling crack. People smoked crack so obviously someone had to sell it to them. Even she knew it was safer than robbing folks.

"These shits is good B!" Manny announced when Trouble made it back. He was far too hungry to wait with that good grease and good aroma seeping through the paper bag. He had eaten half his wings and most of his fries when he made it back.

"The spot on Ogden is better," he replied and dug into his own greasy paper bag. Everything on Ogden was better have him tell it. The girls were definitely prettier and starting to take notice of him with every new outfit he rocked. Plus he was always with Buddha and that's a hell of an endorsement in Highbridge.

"So you gonna put me on or what?" Manny reiterated. The 'or what' was the pistol in his pocket that he was going to rob his old friend with.

"Let's ride..." he said and hopped from the steps. Trouble wanted to stunt and hail a cab but being broke his whole life made stunting hard to do. He would much rather keep his money in his pocket than blow it by showing off. Spendthrifts are the brothers of the devil he once heard and it's true.

Just another of the tacit lessons taught by Buddha. He stayed fresh but wasn't flashy like some of the others. Meanwhile Rip added pieces of jewelry every other week. They set off on foot until they reached the mile high steps on 167th street and began to climb.

"Just let me do the talking..." Trouble urged when they crossed Nelson ave. He was glad to see Buddha was up in the park that oversaw the gas below while Rip was on the ground with the crew. He felt the heat from Rip daily so he was glad they were separated so he could make his pitch.

"Bet," Manny nodded since he didn't know what to say anyway.

"How are your peeps yo?" Buddha asked when he saw them approach. He knew he went to check on his grandmother and respected him for it. His sharp mind immediately placed the other face with him in an instant and cracked a smile.

"She's good. This my um, Manny," he replied, stopping short of giving him a label. They were once forced by hunger to unite to do stick ups but Trouble wasn't hungry anymore. Now it was his sense of loyalty that made him make the introduction. It also made his soul flutter but he didn't know why.

"Sup yo?" Buddha asked since he knew they were here for something.

"He tryna get put on?" Trouble announced. He would be cool with, almost relieved with a nah. He would just give him some money from his pocket and send him back on his way.

"I sold for JB over on the Grand Concourse before," Manny declared. Buddha twisted his lips as he contemplated. He never heard of JB but JB never heard of him either. Not yet anyway because his name would one day ring in every borough. He wanted to pull Monte off the streets before the streets got the best of him. With another kid dealing he could let Monte watch out from this spot. It would be a promotion for him and keep him safe.

"Bring back seven fifty," Buddha decided and tossed him a g-pack. "Not a penny less! Any shorts come out your end."

"Word!" Manny cheesed as he accepted the bag filled with vials. It was worth more than he ever held in his hands in this life. He and Trouble turned to leave before Buddha held them up.

"Yo B," he called and waved him back over. They both stopped so he shooed Manny off and motioned for Trouble.

"Sup yo?" Trouble asked, ready to do whatever he was asked. Literally anything because if you feed a hungry pup he will be your dog for life.

"He's on you B. You brought him here," Trouble reminded. "Your responsibility."

"Word," he paused like he was about to change his mind. His head nodded and ran to catch up with Manny. True to his word the hungry kid rushed around making sales as soon as they reached the spot. Even Rip was impressed since he was making more money for him to blow. A couple hours later he turned in exactly seven fifty and had as much money as his best lick and he was hooked.

"Hmp?" Buddha thought as he watched from above. It was the perfect vantage point to keep watch over the operations and still have some separation. The elevated position allowed him to see up and down 167th as well as Ogden. A refs whistle would pause operations when the rare patrol car cruised by. He could even toss G-packs down to the workers once they ran out.

"Sup yo?" Trouble asked from his side. That's where he spent more of his time lately since Rip was busy spending and fucking.

"Tryna see now..." he said and strained to hear from above. There was too much city noise to hear the conversation so he would just watch and see how it played out.

"Where Rip?" Tonya demanded when she arrived at the spot.

"Ion know who that is," Manny shot back even though he did. He was here to sell crack, not give directions or skip tracing. "You tryna shop or what?"

"Nah cuz, we got an agreement!" she said loud enough to bring Buddha down from the park above. "I put in work! He was supposed to...Hey Buddha! Tell them I put in work! With Black..."

"Give her five caps, on me!" he declared. Manny hit him with a 'yeah right' look and backed off. He wasn't far removed from being broke and hungry everyday so he wasn't coming off anything for free. It still broke his heart to have to turn in the proceeds from each G-pack to get another. Turning in the money he made just didn't sit well with his black soul.

"I got you ma," Big Hank said and stepped up to serve her. He wanted to make sure he got comped for them though so he told Buddha, "Remember these five."

"I got you B," he assured him then spoke up to reassure her. "Anytime she comes she gets five on me! Her money is no good here!"

Everyone looked at Buddha, then to each other to figure out what just happened. None of them were privy to the fact that she lured Tone-Capone and Black Bob into the death trap that killed one of them. Not yet anyway because if nothing was done soon the whole hood would know. Buddha took off so suddenly Trouble got worried and wanted to follow. He vacillated between watching his bosses back or minding his business.

"About to smoke one, sell four and go back and get me

WE RUN NEW YORK

five more!" Tonya schemed like a true crackhead as she hoofed it back into the projects.

She was so locked in on the crack vials in her pocket that she didn't hear the footsteps quickly approaching from her rear. The long, dark walkway up into the project had hosted plenty of murders since it was long and dark.

The window of opportunity could be shut at any moment if someone happened to be coming down. It was closing quickly as she neared the top and the busy courtyard it ended into. Another few feet and it would be closed for now. Buddha couldn't afford later so he lunged and wrapped his arm around her neck.

"Here! Take em..." Tonya grunted when she felt the pressure that cut off her air. She assumed it was a robbery for her rocks and had no intention on dying for them. Especially when as she explained, "Take em, I get, them for, free..."

Buddha kept his eyes locked ahead as he squeezed the life out of her. Rip's mistake could cost them both twenty five to life. It was inevitable that she would eventually get locked up for something or another and use the murder as a 'get out of jail free' card. He heard females approaching but she hadn't gone limp just yet.

"Grrrrr!" Buddha growled and squeezed so hard he passed gas. The voices and laughter grew closer as the girls approached. He recognized the one voice that could make this situation worse and squeezed harder. The only thing worse than letting her go would be being seen killing her.

"Girl Phil got a big ole dick!" Mia bragged on her new man.

"Word?" Lisa asked even though she had slept with him too and it wasn't all that. Chicks will brag on the dick if they like you. But as soon as they fall out they're telling everyone who will listen about your tiny dick.

"Had my ass like..." she was saying just as they rounded the bend. Another few feet and they would clearly see the murder in motion. A empty forty ounce bottle hurled in the air and crashed right in front of their feet, The pause was just enough for Tonya to go limp after Buddha squeezed the life out of her neck. The body on the ground distracted them from the figure springing down the hill in the darkness.

"Girl that's Tonya!" Lisa announced. They both looked ahead, back and around before continuing to the bodega.

"Had my ass climbing the walls..." Mia went on just as Buddha ran smack into Trouble.

"The fuck you doing up here?" Buddhasnapped. Not just because he may have witnessed a murder but would have been one since he wasn't from Highbridge.

"I wanted to watch your back!" he whined like he was in trouble. "The way you took off, I..."

"Come on shorty," Buddha now knew the bottle didn't come from the heavens. Trouble just saved his ass. He sighed and pulled him back towards his building. They cut through the path between the school and the big park to come out on the other side.

Both saw Monte and Alva heading down into the playground but pretended not to. Trouble long ago saw the movement between the two. Buddha had already warned him about giving or selling the woman anything. Rip's mom must have some really good pussy since Monte was risking his life over it.

CHAPTER 17

"Puta madre!" Giggles fussed when the count didn't count up to what it should have counted up to, once again.

"Que?" Miguel wondered since he liked to know which particular mother fucker he meant. Especially when counting money. Which was why he personally involved himself in counting it.

"Alejandro. Alejandro from the Bronx," he clarified since they had several Alejandros in their company. One in Queens, another in lower Manhattan plus a fourth out in Brooklyn.

"Short again?" the boss asked since it was becoming more frequent and more short. The man used the robbery to skim a few extra Gs but it got good to him and he couldn't stop. "How much?"

"Like, fuck you short," Giggles giggled since it meant he might get to bust his gun. Busting his gun always made him giddy. "He puts the right amount on the paper, then it's like, ten percent short!"

It was actually closer to fifteen percent short since Giggles took a pinch off the top himself when he could get away with it. Why not enrich himself off the next man's theft. Especially when he got to bust his gun as a result.

There was no honor amongst thieves and even less with drug dealers. It is not possible to have much honor when you wallow in the same misery you create. The dope fiends leaned courtesy of the good dope they put out. The crack heads destroyed their families and selves to smoke their product. No honor indeed. They had no idea rappers would one day rap about selling and using drugs. They should have though since a generation was growing up amongst crack vials and syringes.

"Mi hermano," Miguel said sadly and shook his head. He mourned since the two men went way back to the island. The man's children called him uncle even though they weren't blood. Not that blood would have saved him. It didn't stop him from stealing so it wouldn't save his life.

"Say the word papi!" Giggles begged and began to stand. He was ready to head over to the Bronx right then and put in work on the spot. Especially since he stood to inherit the lucrative territory for himself.

"He's in Highbridge right?" Miguel asked even though he knew. Giggles opened his mouth to respond but Jennifer suddenly appeared from the rear. Neither noticed she did that anytime she heard Buddha's name or even borough. She knew the deadly game she was playing so she kept ears and eyes open.

"Papi, can I go shopping?" she asked and bounced excitedly. It was a reasonable reason to interrupt since she was always shopping. The bounce set her fine frame into fluid motion.

WE RUN NEW YORK

"Ay Dios mio!" Giggles grunted when he saw what the girl was wearing. The tiny shorts were pulled up into her crotch, showing off her fat rabbit. Giggles knew he fucked up with the outburst and braced himself. He once saw Miguel pistol whip a man into a coma for less than that, over his daughter.

"Tranqilo," Miguel calmly chided him and patted his hand before he responded to her. "Sure. Ju have money?"

"Si papi!" she replied since she had plenty. Not only did both parents keep her designer bags filled, Buddha had just broken her off after breaking her off. The couple grand he slid her way wasn't for the sex. He was still eternally grateful for her changing his life for the better. A man doesn't realize full manhood until he experiences two of life's greatest tests. The first is when he falls in love, the second is when he has his heart broken.

Giggles made a point of not looking at all that ass jiggling away as Jennifer headed back down the hall. Not that he needed to since the fat pussy print was forever embedded on his mind. He turned back to Miguel to finish the talk but the boss changed the subject by sticking his gun in his face. The huge hole in the tip of the 45 staring back at him looked like the Holland tunnel this close up.

"Por que?" Giggles wondered since he had been on the other side of this scenario enough to know how it turned out. It usually ends in a mess that takes hours to clean up.

"Ju want to fuck my daughter?" Miguel asked in a murderous whisper. Unlike some killers he was quiet and let his gun make all the noise. "Have her suck ju dick like some, some puta off the street?"

"Huh?" he reeled at the crazy question. Of course he wanted to fuck his daughter and of course he wanted her to suck his dick, but he wasn't going to tell him that. "Boss, I respect you! You are my family! She is my family!"

"Ay Dios mio papi! What are ju doing!" Jennifer reeled when she came out as her father pressed the barrel to his cheek. One tug on the trigger would have changed the wall color from gaudy Puerto Rican yellow to sickening blood and brains pink.

"I respect your daughter. I respect you. I would never dishonor you papi," Giggles declared valiantly. Even lifted his head to make sure the bullet reached his brain. You can't kill as many people as he killed and be afraid of death. The appeal seemed to give Miguel pause so he drove it home for the whole family since Esmeralda had come to investigate as well. "I would honor her, marry her! Never disrespect her!"

"Tranqilo Miguel," his wife urged. She was moved by the sentiment plus didn't want her new furniture ruined with brain matter. Add the fact that she knew a boss when she saw one. Giggles was one in the making. Perfect for giving her daughter the same lavish life she was accustomed to. He was her choice for Jennifer even if Jennifer had chosen another.

"Hmp?" Miguel hummed for a moments contemplation. The gun came down when he made his decision. He dismissed his women before resuming. "Alejandro huh?"

"Si," Giggles agreed with a nod and slight giggle. He took his first breath of his new life since being spared was like being born again. "I'll go handle it now."

"No," Miguel decided and sat him back down. "Send the black kid. Buddha, they owe us one."

"Ok," he replied and pulled his phone to send the order that would send slugs at the thief. Miguel went back to counting and missed the murderous side eye glance Giggles gave. The man should have known not to put a gun up someone's nostril and not shoot. He loved that man but he just broke his heart. "It's set."

"Let me know when, so I can send flowers..." Miguel announced and continued the count.

※

"Yo! That shit is ill B!" Manny cheered when he saw the new medallion swinging from the new chain around Rip's neck. Rip still really didn't like the kids Buddha put down but Manny got cool points when he acknowledged his new jewels. Buddha pretended not to even see the new piece when they were packaging up their daily G-packs. If anything it pissed him off because his so-called partner wasn't pulling his weight.

"Word up! Stay down and you gonna be shining too shorty," Rip assured him and passed his personal blunt. A year ago four or five of them would smoke on the same blunt but these days it was each man for his own blunt. The kid took the customer two pulls and passed before going back to slinging the vials that provided his daily bread.

"Can't wait!" Manny shouted back and twisted his lips since he didn't want to wait. It still burned him up to turn in three times as much as he got to keep. "I'm the one out here slinging this shit..."

"Huh?" Monte asked when he heard the kid mumbling to himself.

"Who? Nah, I'm just saying. Nawmean..." he rambled sufficiently enough for Monte to dismiss him and go back to his own sales. He was seeing more money lately since Alva had cut down on her smoking. Love is like that since it can change hearts and habits. Luckily for him that meant she wanted to fuck more and he didn't mind fucking her. Especially since she wasn't charging him anymore. She was still costing though since it cost to maintain a woman, and Alva was his woman.

"A-yo Trouble!" Buddha called from the park above the gas station. Once the kid looked up he waved him up. "Come-mere B!"

Trouble looked over at Manny before taking off. He didn't like leaving his post but the boss called so he went running. Rip hadn't been out all night so Buddha was working double. He was more interested in the money while Rip preferred the things money could buy. Like gold, denim, diamonds and vagina.

"Sup yo," he asked in a hush when he reached Buddha. The look in the man's eyes told him this was something serious.

"I need you to watch my back again," he said and paused for him to remember the last time he watched his back while he choked the life out of Tonya.

"Word!" he agreed instantly. Had Buddha given the word and a gun Trouble would have marched over to 164th street and laid Alejandro out on the spot. He didn't though since that was exactly what he planned to do himself. He had instructions and planned to follow them to the letter. Especially after the half botched job they did with the Black Bob hit. The irony of murdering a man for robbing the man he was about to murder made him shake his head.

He stopped at the payphone in front of the garage and made a call that set another call in motion. If all went according to plan he would be in and out as easily as the cop and go traffic at the spot. Trouble noticed the paper bag in his hand by the way he clutched it close.

Trouble had a lot of questions but kept them to himself. Even he felt his mentor get colder as they crossed over 165th street. A chill he could literally feel just walking next to him. His eyes narrowed into slits as the 164th street got closer with every step. Buddha took note of the young Spanish workers out slinging caps. Meanwhile Alejandro talked in rapid fire Spanish on a payphone. Neither understood the pleas and explanations as Buddha closed in.

"Mi hermano! No! Never!" Alejandro pleaded into the phone. It was all lies since yeah, he did.

"Yes my brother, ju did. Ju stole," Miguel assured him. If he wasn't sure death wouldn't be on his heels. "I sent a driver to get ju. He will be there any second."

Alejandro had no intention of waiting for a driver to come take him to his death. He had plenty of money put up so he hung up and turned to make his getaway. Except he turned right into Buddha.

"Get out of..." Alejandro was saying while the paper bag was coming up. When it was parallel with his face the gun within roared and ruined his statement. Trouble froze for a moment until he saw Buddha never broke his pace. He rushed to catch up as Alejandro's workers looked away. Some had been warned, the others hadn't signed up for this part of the game.

Buddha dumped the pistol out of the bag and into a dumpster. The bag prevented him from leaving prints or it from leaving gunpowder residue on his hand. Even he had to nod at how proficient Giggles murder game was. His tongue went to the chipped tooth and he was glad he didn't have to tangle with him.

CHAPTER 18

"Where's Manny?" Trouble asked and looked around again and didn't see him.

"Went to the bodega," Big Hank answered since he gave the kid money for some snacks himself. His grumbling stomach scrunched his face curiously since it was still grumbling. "That was a while ago tho?"

"He's gone," E-baby announced matter of factly. Everyone looked to him for an explanation so he explained. "Son had that look in his. Almost like these crackheads, but different. The same tho..."

"Word," Joey cosigned and he would know since he saw that look every time he looked in the mirror. He was just smart enough to come up with a scheme to steal without getting caught.

"I'ma bust that nigga," Trouble declared, proving he wasn't ready to bust nothing. Because if you're gonna kill a nigga, you just kill him. No need for an announcement. Fuck around and hear that same announcement at your trial.

"Fuck that shit B. He sold himself for a G," E-baby advised.

"Not even a G since he got to keep two fiddy. Nigga sold himself way short!" Joey added. They may have been done with it but Rip had something to say about it. It was Buddha's idea to put them on so he had to throw it back in his face.

"Yeah, and since that's your man, you gotta cover that short!" Rip declared. Trouble glanced up to where Buddha would usually be perched but he was out with Jennifer.

"A'ight," he nodded. He had a few Gs put up and could cover the loss.

"Now nigga! We ain't closing out with no shorts B!" Rip shot back. Buddha did like to make sure all dollars were counted and accounted for at the end of each night. He was still shutting down at a certain time so Kev in the projects could eat. As well as the thugs on 170th since he wasn't in position to go to war with anyone. Business just boomed even more during the hours they were out.

"Bull shit, crab ass, sucker ass..." Trouble groaned as he headed up 167th to go home. Those stairs are a lot easier to go down than they were up but an idea crossed his mind halfway down. That meant turning around and running back up. It was a long shot and that only made him sprint that much faster. He bust a left on Nelson and ran over to 164th and turned right.

Much to Giggles dismay someone else was given the spot Alejandro just vacated. His blood was still on the sidewalk and that was a good sign. A few of the dealers noticed Trouble as he rushed by and turned back on University.

"Yes!" Trouble cheered and pumped his fist when he saw the dumpster hadn't been dumped yet. The triumph was short lived when he saw a whole day's worth of more garbage was piled on top. "Fuck!"

Fuck is right because that's a lot of garbage. Plus, New York city garbage isn't like other garbage. It was filled with dirty diapers, crack vials and used syringes, contaminated with everything under the sun. And a few guns since he found a nine millimeter a few minutes in. It would have saved him some time but was missing its clip. He dug on until he found what he was looking for. The pistol Buddha used to murder Alejandro was destined for the dump, never to be seen again. Until he put it into another bag and tucked it under his arm and pressed on.

Trouble crossed back over on 165th and sprinted back over to the steps. His mind moved even faster than his feet and he found himself on Jerome avenue before he was ready. He tried to talk himself into what he needed to do but still hadn't.

"He sold himself for a G," he repeated like E-baby had said. Then nodded at what Joey said since it was only seven fifty. "Seven hundred and fifty dollars out of my damn stash!"

"Is that you Sean?" his weary grandmother called when she heard the front door opening. The boy was trouble but she still called him by his birth name from time to time. Hopefully the sweet young boy he once was would answer one of those times. Hopefully but not likely because once the streets get hold of you it's hard to let go.

"Yeah grandma," he called back and closed the door behind him before heading into the living room. "You good ma? Need some money?"

"Yes baby, and no. I still have some left from last time," she replied, sighed and continued. "You have to be careful. Elizabeth said some boys came looking for her Manny. They had knives!"

"Hmp," he huffed since he was looking for him too but he had a gun. A gun that even he knew he wouldn't use. He couldn't, so he would tuck it away on the old stash spot on the roof. "Ok ma."

He agreed since he was being as careful as he could. Selling drugs in the Bronx is one of the most dangerous professions on the planet but still a lot safer than being a stick up kid. He rushed into his room and nodded at the new clothes and sneakers that replaced the old, beat up gear he used to rock. He sat his old clothes and sneakers on the sidewalk and they became someone's new clothes and sneakers.

His head nodded because he was winning and E-baby was right, fuck that shit. He dug his stash out and counted out the seven fifty he had to replace. The setback summoned another sigh but there was still plenty left over. Especially since he started from less than zero. Being born in the hood isn't ground level, it's six feet under.

Trouble had softened his tone by the time he left the apartment. He and Manny had in deed came from less than zero. Without enough of nothing kids needs to grow into respectable adults. At least he had the love of a grandmother. Manny's mother loved the life and the lights and her son was just a byproduct of that. Extra baggage she sat down years ago. He hopped up the rest of the steps and came out on the roof. He looked and listened to make sure the coast was clear from smokers and lovers before headed over to the vent that doubled as their stash. He and Manny kept all kinds of trinkets and treasures there over the years so he was semi surprised to see it empty.

"Damn B," he laughed at the emptiness Manny left

behind. He smiled at the reasoning that Manny had no reason to come back since it was empty. That made it a perfect spot to hide the gun. He eased it into the hole and secured the cover before turning around and running straight past the last person he expected to see.

"What's that B?" Manny asked with that same look in his eye E-baby spoke of and Joey confirmed.

"Nothing now," he sighed and turned to retrieve the gun since he now saw the look in his eyes for himself. Manny tried to get a peak at what he was doing but he tucked it away before he could. He marched over here with the intention of killing him but now just wanted to get away from him as soon as possible. "I'm out!"

"Word B? It's like that? You really bugging cuz I hit them niggas up?" he asked as Trouble tried to get past him. He was actually mad that Trouble wasn't mad about the trouble he caused.

"You hit me up too son! I'm with the Buddha crew! That's my mans and them B!" he shot back and puffed his chest out. He may have been proud of his loyalty but Manny found it amusing.

"Yo, you sound like a real dick rider right now B!" he laughed without a hint of merriment. In fact it was closer to sinister than benevolent. Trouble tried to keep walking so he grabbed his arm. He couldn't just let his only friend leave him like that. "Hold up yo!"

"Get the fuck off me!" he growled and knocked his hand away. "That's some sucker shit you did and now I gotta pay that shit back tonight!"

"So, you got a G on you right now?" Manny asked as that devilish look twinkled in his eyes. He looked down at the bulge in Trouble's pocket and nodded. "Yeah you do..."

There was a tense few seconds that felt like an eternity as the two friends contemplated their next move. Being friends as long as they had made them move the same at the same time. Time slowed as both went for the guns in their waistbands. Ironically they played QuickDraw cowboy on this same roof many times as they grew up.

Manny was usually faster and was the first to say 'boom, you're dead' when he popped his cap pistol. Except these were real pistols with real bangs and real bullets. Manny once again beat his friend in pulling his weapon. Trouble was a split second later getting his shot off.

Manny fired first but his aim was off. His slug sailed harmlessly by and slammed into the next building. Trouble's shot was dead on and knocked Manny off his feet. It tore through his cheek and stretched him out on the ground.

"You got that B," Manny surrendered through his shattered jaw since he dropped his gun. Trouble nodded in agreement since he indeed had it. He turned to walk off and leave him alive. Manny planned to grab his gun and shoot him in his back before he got away. Trouble must have felt that and stopped short. He spun and looked down at his old friend who was now his enemy.

"On second thought..." he thought and pointed the gun at his forehead. A tug on the trigger ended their friendship once and for all. A slight smirk turned up the corner of his mouth as he lowered the gun. Now he finally got the chance to say, "Bang, you're dead."

"Wow! Word? Wow!" Buddha reeled as he digested the kids' revelation. He looked at him again to see if he saw a killer but couldn't quite see it. Until he squinted and saw that familiar glint in his iris. The same one he saw in his own after he whacked Tonya and again after Alejandro. Black Rob was a spur of the moment thing and doesn't quite count. One doesn't become an actual killer until they set off to murder and murder. "You didn't have to do that B? It's just a G?"

"Seven fifty," he corrected as he had been corrected. "Yes I did tho. Son tried us. You put the nigga on, on the strength of me. I did have to."

"Word," the boss agreed because he was right after all. "You can't even be nice to a nigga in this game since niggas take compassion as weakness. Niggas don't even respect giving them a pass so you have to kill them."

Both went silent to bask in the afterglow of his words. Buddha already knew it, but saying it made it law. Hearing it was confirmation because Manny would have gunned him down if he hadn't killed him first.

"I'm ready to make sales B!" Trouble decided out loud. He was getting two hundred dollars a day just for being the lookout but wanted more. Not necessarily more money, just more responsibility, more juice.

"That's a demotion my nigga. Once this shit pop we gonna have other niggas working for us! All y'all coming in from out the cold!" Buddha explained. He had plans for expansion in the very near future. Rip appeared in the big park and Trouble already knew to spread out. Not just because grown folks were about to talk, he knew Rip wasn't feeling him.

"Get lost little nigga," Rip demanded even though the kid was already leaving. Buddha smiled since he got a kick out of it. "What's good B? Your little mans told you his peeps ran off with a G-pack?"

"Yeah. He took care of it," Buddha said, referring to paying for the short. The murder would be their secret.

"So bust it, the little nigga Zero pushed up on me. Said him and Bam wanna get down with us," he happily reported.

"What you say?" Buddha asked to test his intelligence.

"Told em come the fuck on! Shit they already got the projects. They can push our shit up there," he said and had the audacity to shrug his shoulders, like it was just that simple.

"Here..." Buddha said and pulled his gun.

"Fuck you giving me that for? You know I stay strapped like a jap!" he replied even though no one knows just how strapped a jap really is. The shit rhymes so they went with it.

"Cool, so go murk Kev so we can take his spot," Buddha replied and mocked his shrug since that wasn't just that simple either. Killing Kev would just be the start of many more killings. He was University Homes' own and they wouldn't take it lying down. The White building had a few killers but they wouldn't ride on some personal beef and the Buddha crew didn't have enough manpower to fight anyone. Not yet anyway.

"Kill Kev?" Rip reeled making it sound as crazy as it was supposed to sound. Almost as crazy as just sending work with Kev's workers and thinking that too wouldn't start some shit.

"Gonna have to if you talking about bum rushing his spot," he explained.

"So, Zero can't come work for us if he wants? Kev don't

own the nigga!" he shot back. Buddha had to squint at him to finally see that his friend wasn't that bright.

"Yeah, he do. He own the projects, he own the project niggas!" Buddha snapped but caught his tone. "We can get Kev to buy from us, then he working for us and don't even know it,"

"Word," Rip agreed even though he didn't get it yet. "We got a good connect for the low."

"Shit, we need to re-up soon anyway," he reminded since Rip didn't focus on the business part of the business. He just liked the money. If it hadn't been for Buddha's extra investment they would not be moving up the food chain.

"Word, I need to pull some cash out tho," Rip requested. "Need some BBSs for the whip..."

"B? You was already short on the first re-up! We tryna double up next time! Ain't no room to spend shit!" he fussed. Once again Buddha had to check his tone since no one likes getting barked at. "Once we up we can ball the fuck out. See Ion buy shit! Still wearing these raggedy ass shell toes!"

"Cuz you a cheap nigga son! That's why you only keep one broad cuz yo cheap ass don't wanna spend no bread!" Rip cackled.

"Word!" Buddha laughed at the lie. Being cheap had nothing to do with why he only saw Jennifer. That had everything to do with love.

CHAPTER 19

"Something is different? Ju are different?" Esmeralda Camacho asked and squinted at her daughter across the table to see if she could see it. She couldn't but she was sure something was different. The girl had become a woman. "Si, definitely different!"

"Por que mami?" Jennifer asked since she was sure her mother hadn't noticed her ass had gotten fatter from the months of back shots she was getting from across the bridge. Even she noticed her own lips were fuller after discovering how much she loved to suck dick. Quite accidentally actually since Buddha had gotten so proficient at eating pussy she felt like she owed him one so she returned the favor. She discovered she was able to make her man move and squirm like a puppet master controls his puppet when she had him in her mouth.

The good sex was made better since they were head over heels in love with each other. Young love is the best love but add in first love and this was true love. A wise man once said, 'Love whom you love mildly, perhaps he will become hateful to you someday. Hate whom you hate mildly, perhaps he will become your beloved someday'

"Mmhm..." her mother hummed like a threat. She knew the girl was up to something since she certainly was at that age. A young Esmeralda was fucking real good by the time she was seventeen and her daughter had just turned eighteen. No way she wasn't getting some dick from somewhere no matter what she said. She would find out eventually so for now she nodded and inhaled the wonderful aromas of the restaurant wafting in the air. The same smells reached Jennifer but she didn't smile like her mother. Instead she winced, and began to turn green.

"Ugh," Jennifer grunted and wretched like she might throw up. Her mother tilted her head curiously and watched as she tried to keep it together.

"Ju better not!" Esmeralda growled as her child struggled to keep her breakfast from splashing on the lunch table. The waitress brought out a sheep head for the next table and that was all she wrote. Jennifer jumped up and tore off for the ladies room. "Ju better not be!"

"Agh! Ugh! Ewww!" Jennifer wretched and upchucked what was left from breakfast. She stood from the commode and turned to leave the stall. Except her stomach wasn't quite done so she turned back into the bowl and threw up some more.

She went to the sink and washed her face and mouth while looking at her reflection. Her eyes were watery from throwing up and her throat burned. Her stomach was still doing flips and flutters but she lifted her chin and marched back out to the table like nothing had happened.

"Jour pregnant! Ay Dios mio! How? I know how so, who?"

Esmeralda insisted. The revelation caught Jennifer so off guard she almost forgot she wasn't a virgin.

"Ju 'buggin mami! How could I be..." she was saying until the image of Buddha on top of her and inside of her with his face twisted and contorted as he bust so many nuts inside of her.

"Bente!" Esmeralda shouted as she came around and snatched her from her booth.

"What are ju doing mami!" Jennifer pleaded as her mother snatched her from the restaurant. Giggles got out of the car in a rush, ready to bust something when he saw them hit the sidewalk and look around frantically.

"Get back in the car!" Esmeralda shouted as she looked around. He complied and she found what she was looking for.

Jennifer was still complaining as her mother pulled her across the street and into a pharmacy. She drugged her up and down the aisles until she conceded she couldn't find what she was looking for. All that was left was to march over to the counter and pound her diamond laced hand on the glass.

"Can I help you?" the clerk asked with a strained smile on her face. If she had a dollar for every time one of these spoiled rich folks pounded on the glass she wouldn't have to work here anymore.

"We need the test! With the plus sign!" Esmeralda demanded. The clerk initially thought she wanted a covid test until she saw the embarrassment on her daughter's face.

"One sec..." she said and turned to retrieve a pregnancy test. The pregnancy test was the most shoplifted item in the store even though the huge condom display was placed right inside the front door. "Directions on the back."

"Where is ju bathroom!" The woman demanded and almost got denied. Except she tossed a crispy hundred dollar bill on the counter that granted her access to the employee's only bathroom.

"Mami!" Jennifer pleaded and tried to pull away. All it did was drive her mother's fingernails even deeper into her flesh. She pushed her into a stall and scrambled to open the package.

"Take jour pants down!" she shouted when she saw the girl hadn't budged. All that kung fu, karate and jujitsu didn't have shit on an angry mama. Jennifer didn't want that smoke and let out a loud sigh as she pulled down her pants and panties. "Pee!"

"Ok mami!" she whined. She reached for the test strip but Esmeralda wasn't going for it.

"Ju might miss..." she explained as her daughter got a good stream going. She ignored the warm pee on her fingers as she held it under.

Esmeralda looked at her diamond studded Rolex and started the countdown while Jennifer wiped and pulled her clothes back up. She thought about making a run for it when she couldn't recall her last period. There was no pause on her visits to the Bronx several times a week. Buddha was just as addicted to her insides as she was addicted to the dick being inside of her.

"Aaaaaah!" Esmeralda screamed so shrill the windows rattled.

"Uh-oh," the clerk said when she heard it from the front of the store. She knew that sound well enough to know the test results.

"Un-uh mami! That thing don't work!" Jennifer insisted when her mother shoved the plus sign into her face.

"Don't make this worse by lying," the woman said calmly as she unerringly calmed down. The seriousness in her tone gave the girl a shiver through her soul. "Who did it? Who are ju sleeping with?"

"I'm not mami, I..." she tried but cried before she could finish the lie. She wiped her tears, puffed out her chest and declared, "He loves me! I love him! I'm not telling ju!"

"And jour father is going to kill him!" Esmeralda warned. "He will find out and kill him!"

Jennifer knew her father was a killer and had no doubt he would kill Buddha. The revelation turned the tears back on. Esmeralda just watched her cry since a river of tears wouldn't save whoever knocked her up.

"Listen chica. If ju really love him do what I say. It's the only way to keep him alive," the mother decided and stuck her own chest out. She didn't care about whoever knocked her up but knew it would destroy the girl if he was murdered. He would definitely be murdered so she had a plan.

✦

"When you gonna let son know you fucking his daughter?" Rip asked as he drove across the bridge to Harlem. "I know she sucking that dick! I had this Haitian bitch the other night! Son!"

"Word," Buddha replied just to keep the conversation moving as they moved through Manhattan. He was totally preoccupied with the fact that he hadn't heard from Jennifer in two days. That was rare since they spent every night on the phone. Now hers just rang and his didn't.

"Pussy was like, a thousand degrees B! I think that's how

she burnt me?" he wondered as he rambled but Buddha didn't hear a word of it. "I know her ass better not pop up saying she pregnant! These bitches be buggin yo! Nut in 'em in a couple times and they come back talmbout, they pregnant!"

"Word," he offered like the spare change one passes off to a panhandler. He was relieved to see the familiar faces of Miguel's crew as they neared the block. He saw even more of them, just not the one he was looking for. In fact, quite a few faces were missing.

"I see Javier out here..." Rip said and pulled into a vacant spot on the curb.

There was no need for pistols on this block so they left them inside and grabbed the bag full of cash. They could feel the weight of all the eyes on them from every direction but Buddha looked up to the window he knew to belong to his woman. He hoped to see her smiling back but was not to be.

"The Bronx in this muthafucka!" Javier cheered as a greeting when he saw them approaching. He knew why they were here so he stood to take them inside the building.

"Sup B?" Buddha asked but he really meant, 'where is everybody?' Not only was the love of his life missing but he didn't see Miguel or his pet psycho Giggles anywhere.

"You my nigga," Javier said over his shoulder as they passed through the lobby and walked up the stairs. Buddha assumed he would see Miguel and Giggles inside but neither man was present amongst the men inside the apartment.

"Where is Miguel?" Rip asked. It was a start so Buddha listened intently when he answered.

"In Puerto Rico. His daughter is getting married," he replied and asked his own question. "How many you guys from the Bronx getting?"

"Four!" Rip answered proudly. He may have wanted to trick off the money as soon as they made it but was glad Buddha had some business sense. If they kept flipping and moving up they could move up to moving weight. Rip wanted to run Highbridge but his partner had loftier goals. Buddha wanted to run New York.

"His daughter?" Buddha managed to ask in hopes he had another daughter in Puerto Rico. Even though he knew Jennifer to be an only child as far as she knew of anyway. That still made more sense than her marrying anyone. Especially since they were just together a couple days ago.

"Jennifer," Javier replied and Buddha didn't hear another word. He watched through a fog of hurt and confusion as Javier counted the money then passed it off to the next man to count it again. No one wanted to take any chances after what happened to Alejandro. Even if they had no idea it was Buddha who made it happen to him.

"You good B?" Rip finally asked out of concern.

"Yeah, why you ask me that!" Buddha snapped. It was only then that he realized they were back in the car headed back over to the Bronx.

"Cuz you zoned out son!" Rip replied. It was just then when his brain finally caught up with the earlier conversation. "I know you not stressed cuz your jump off done got married!"

"Who?" he asked who he was talking to even though they were the only ones in the car. Rip ran through chicks like he changed his drawers so they didn't mean much to him. Which is why he couldn't understand the dull ache in his friend's chest that felt like he was dying. Which is one of the worst parts of a broken heart. It doesn't actually kill you so you have to live with it, and that can be worse.

"See, that's why I be on my, 'fuck a bitch, then fuck the bitch'. Stick and move my dude!" Rip comforted. It was no comfort though because only two things can cure a broken heart. Time and new pussy. The time just started ticking and Buddha needed to find out what was really going on before he went in pursuit of new pussy.

CHAPTER 20

"I am literally gonna tear this ass up!" Giggles vowed as he kissed his hand and crossed his heart. It had to be divine intervention that delivered the fine, young thing he had been lusting after for years. Her father put a gun in his face for looking at her ass, and now he was about to tear that ass up.

He couldn't believe his good fortune when Esmeralda told him he was going to marry her daughter. He readily accepted even though Jennifer hadn't said a word. She looked like she was being forced but he didn't mind since he was going to force his dick way up inside of her. Plus the added incentive of being part of the family put him one step closer to what he wanted to be. He wanted to be the boss and now was in position to inherit the whole organization. Miguel would have to die for him to inherit the throne but everyone dies.

Miguel spent lavishly on the last minute, mountainside wedding but Jennifer was mentally a million miles away. All she wanted was her Buddha but a dead Buddha was no good to anyone. She would go through with it for now until she could figure something else out. Esmeralda insisted they keep Giggles in the dark for her own reasons. She figured once the handsome hunk of Latin man slid up inside her daughter she would be hooked. They wouldn't even have to tell him she was already pregnant.

Jennifer had to be asked twice during the ceremony if she took that man to be her lawful husband before she huffed a curt, 'yeah'. She did find out his name was actually Herman and that got a giggle out of her. He got her cheek to kiss when the preacher pronounced them man and wife.

Miguel ran the drug family but his wife ran the real one. When she told him about the nuptials he initially protested about his daughter marrying a thug. She of course reminded him that her father once said the same thing. Then pressed the fact that he trusted the man with their safety so who better to maintain and protect Jennifer as her husband.

All that led them to the secluded villa high in the mountains. The view from the balcony was breathtaking but all Giggles wanted to do was bend her over the rail and fuck her. If he could only get her to come out of the bathroom.

"Fuck!" he cursed and barged over to kick the door open. He stopped just short when he remembered she was his wife. He couldn't be a brute and treat her like he treated other chicks. Chicks like Rosalinda who was probably the most confused of all the wedding guests. He calmed and gently tapped on the door and asked, "Are you ok?"

'Am I ok? Mi madre force me to marry some man I don't love when I'm in love with my Buddha' she moaned internally. The thought of her murderous father murdering her Buddha made her sigh. She would go along with the plan for now. She wiped her tears and pulled the door open.

"Are you ok?" he asked again since the distress was obvious on her face. He wanted to hurdle whatever obstacle was in the way of him getting in that pussy.

"No. My period came on!" she wailed and gripped her rock hard stomach. "I have bad cramps."

"Fuck!" he groaned at his misfortune, not hers. He almost decided to fuck her anyway until his cologne reached her nostrils.

"Agh!" she gagged and ran back into the bathroom to throw up.

"Fuck," Giggles sighed and accepted his fate. He had no idea the girl had some dynamite head so he gave up altogether. "Get some rest. I'm going to get a drink."

"Si," she agreed and frowned until he left the room. It was the first time she had been alone since they left New York. She rushed over to the nightstand for the phone but there wasn't one. She rushed around the room in a frantic search but no phone was to be found. This was a honeymoon suite so they didn't have one. There were no phones, computers or even a TV. Just mirrors on the ceiling, foam wedges for back shots and all kinds of lubes and oils but no phone.

"Fuck!" Jennifer fussed and collapsed on the bed. Meanwhile Rosalinda got a knock on her door.

"Hello?" Rosalinda asked as she neared the door. She expected to be alone since both of her dick donors would be with their wives. She did a double take when she saw Giggles standing on the other side. She pulled the door open, expecting to see her friend by his side but he was alone. "Is everything ok?"

"It will be..." Giggles said as he walked in on top of her. He backed her up until they reached the bed. She fell back and removed her panties while he dropped his pants.

He pulled her thick legs up onto his shoulders and plunged inside. Giggles closed his eyes to pretend he was inside of his pretty wife and took her to pound town.

※

"We are heading back to New Jork," Esmeralda advised when the newlyweds joined the rest of the family for brunch. She hoped Giggles put the dick on the girl real good and fuck her into her senses. Plus it would be a lot easier to put this baby on him since she was only a few weeks along.

Miguel only offered a nod since he was having a hard time thinking about anyone putting the dick on his daughter. Especially the way he used to put the dick on her when they were that age. Rosalinda couldn't look up either since her belly and box was filled to the rim with Giggles' seeds. It was all he could do to go back to the honeymoon suite after dicking her down so good. Jennifer was still fully dressed, cured into a fetal ball on the bed.

"Already!" Jennifer moaned at the thought of being left here with him. Especially with no chance to use a phone to call her Buddha.

"Si. I have a city to run," Miguel reminded. The sound of it made Giggle's heart quake, since he longed to make that claim. He married the boss's daughter which was a step in the right direction.

"Jour papa has business, and so do ju," Esmeralda explained, then turned to her new son in law, "I want some grandbabies!"

"You sure you don't need me?" Giggles asked. He was

ready to get back to New York as well since he was fucking Rosalinda up there already.

"No!" Esmeralda answered for her husband and glared at her daughter. She now knew she gave him the cold shoulder instead of some good, hot Puerto Rican pussy. Jennifer rolled her eyes and crossed her arms over her chest.

"Well, can Rosalinda stay down with us?" Jennifer asked so she would have someone to keep her busy.

"Yes," Giggles answered with enough enthusiasm to draw Esmeralda's eyes. She knew the girl fucked her husband while she shopped and blew his money. The girl could keep getting the dick because she was getting the money.

"Sure," Miguel spoke up and decided the matter. The table morphed into a chorus of forks clicking on plates and bowls while the family ate.

A private jet whisked Miguel and Esmeralda back to New York while Jennifer was left trying to figure out how to dodge the dick and reach her man.

※

"Yo Buddha!" Rip called again and waved a hand in front of his face. They congregated in his apartment to cook coke and tell jokes.

"Son!" he shot back in frustration that had nothing to do with him.

"I know you are not still sweating that broad B! Son, we in New York. Home of the baddest bitches on the planet! I just fucked a Russian bitch B! You ever had some Russian pussy?" he dared. "Shit good as a mufucka! Good and cold!"

"You shot the fuck out B!" Buddha said and got a well

needed laugh. It was the first time he smiled or laughed since Jennifer got ghost on him.

"Y'all be fucking them basic bitches B! All my shorties be exotic!" Joey declared.

"Son, you fucked a dwarf and a fucking albino! The fuck is you talking about, exotic!" Buddha laughed. He was the boss so the crew laughed when he laughed. Plus that shit was funny.

"See, she was a midget yo! There's a big difference son!" Joey replied in defense of his short chick.

"Neither one is big enough to have a big difference!" Rip added and shook his head.

"That's better than that nigga Monte!" Trouble laughed to get in on the session. Part of being in this crew was being able to snap and get snapped on.

"That nigga don't get no pussy!" Rip laughed. "Never has!"

"Yeah he be sneaking off with that chick with the..." the kid was saying while Buddha went wide eyed. He knew Rip would lose his mind if he found out Monte was fucking his mother. If the kid mentioned Alva's distinct orange hair it was up.

"Run over to the bodega and grab me a box of White Owls!" he shouted over the kid. Rip scrunched his face at the fresh box of cigars on the table but didn't question it.

"Bet," the kid said and hopped up to carry out his mission. He rushed off before Buddha could give him money because he liked buying things for his boss to show gratitude for finally having money in his pocket.

"I'll be right back," Buddha declared and headed for the door. Everyone present knew he was going home to call Jennifer. Rip's mother was coming in as he was heading out.

"Sup fellas," Alva smiled as she entered her home. The

greeting was plural but she was smiling towards Monte. That smile invoked a curious frown from Rip when he saw it. He snapped his head towards Monte who was looking away.

"Sup ma," Rip replied and waited for her to crack for some crack since a fresh batch was drying on the table. He had noticed the changes in her appearance for the better but didn't know she had stopped smoking. She had started cooking and eating since she was happy and content.

"Nothing," she smiled and fluttered her eyes at Monte once again but he was still looking away. Meanwhile Buddha rushed inside his own apartment and found his mother on her phone.

"I need to make a call ma!" he urged.

"Then you need to get your own line!" she shot back and went back to cackling with her sister down south. "This boy got a good job, making plenty of money but too cheap to get his own line..."

"Psssssh," he hissed and spun on his heels. He had just paid the phone bill along with all the other bills but couldn't pull rank on his mother. He rushed back out and hit the stairwell. It was too bad Rip wasn't present to verify since he had just beat their joint record in racing down the sixteen flights of steps. He slightly turned and ankle hopping down the stairs but it didn't even slow him down. In fact, seeing someone heading for the nearest payphone only sped him up.

"Gotcha!" he cheered at the old lady he beat to the phone and dropped his quarters.

"Sucka!" the woman fussed and crossed the street to the next phone. Buddha let out a sigh when the phone began to ring. It always rang, but never got answered, until now.

"Hello?" Esmeralda nearly dared when she answered her

daughter's phone. The phone rang every few minutes since she returned from Puerto Rico but she never answered it, until now.

"Hello?" Buddha asked when he didn't recognize the voice. He was ready to hang up and dial again until she spoke up and said her piece.

"I know who ju are! I know what ju did! My daughter is married now!" she insisted forcefully but not loud enough for her husband to hear.

Buddha just blinked and tried to figure out what was going on. He and Jennifer were in love. No way she ran off and married someone else. His heart felt like it was gripped by a large hand that squeezed until his knees buckled. He thought he was having a heart attack but it was just a broken heart. Those can kill too but he lived through it.

"Ju hear me? My daughter is married now! It's over, don't call her anymore!" Esmeralda growled. "Don't call anymore or I will find ju and I will kill ju!"

CHAPTER 21

"Son, I got exactly what you need!" Rip cheered when Buddha pulled his door open. Buddha opened his mouth to ask what it was, exactly that he needed but two pretty white girls followed him inside.

"Word?" Buddha laughed as they marched into his apartment. His mother was out on a date so they had the place to themselves.

"Word. I was down on Delancey street," Rip explained, which explained the how he got the girls. He was down there buying leathers and gold and picked up a couple gold diggers as well. "Darcy and Delilah."

"Uh, Delilah. She's Darcy," one corrected.

"Whatever. Which one you want?" he shrugged. Both girls poked their breasts out as he looked them over. Both were pretty with pretty big breasts so he shrugged and chose.

"Delilah," Buddha chose and took her by the hand.

"I'm out B!" Rip called as he took Darcy out the door and over to his apartment.

"Nice room," Delilah said delightfully when they entered

Buddha's bedroom. Jennifer had him paint the entire room black and ran blue string lighting around the ceiling. Even the large mirror on the wall was her idea so they could watch themselves fuck.

"Thanks," he said and twisted his lips ruefully at the irony of someone else enjoying her design. Those lips twisted the other way at the thought of whoever Jennifer's new husband was enjoying all the sexual tricks he taught her. Delilah moved in for a kiss and took his mind off of his sorrows.

"So..." Rosalinda cheered when she and Jennifer walked in the courtyard of the villa. She was generally nosey but now needed to know why her new husband was in her room every night.

"No," she shot back curtly since she didn't want to talk about it. She only wanted to talk to Buddha but still hadn't gotten a chance to use a phone since someone was always with her.

"Ok chica," Rosalinda shrugged. She hoped she shunned Giggles again tonight so she could ride his dick, backwards. They walked along in silence and nursed their own secrets. Giggles appeared and broke the silence.

"Let's go to San Juan and party!" he declared excitedly. "We are in Puerto Rico, we have to hit the city!"

"Yes!" Rosalinda cheered like it was the best idea she had ever heard. It was actually a great idea as far as Jennifer was concerned as well since she would finally be alone.

"Ju guys go 'head. My cramps..." she begged off and clutched her stomach. Rosalind knew her well enough to know she had mild periods but wasn't going to protest about having Giggles to herself for a few hours. They usually had to settle for quickie blow jobs or back shots, but now they could get to it.

"You sure?" Giggles asked, hoping she was since he wanted some pussy. He would prefer hers but would settle for Rosalinda's.

"Si. Have fun ju guys," she smiled. They both turned to leave but Jennifer had a final request. "Give me jour key so I can watch TV."

Rosalinda happily tossed her the keys as she and Giggles headed out the hotel. They were going to the closest hotel they could find and rent a room for the night since a night of partying was the perfect cover to spend a night under the covers.

"I'm coming, my Buddha!" Jennifer moaned loudly as she rushed up to Rosalinda's room. Her hands shook from excitement as she picked up the phone. She frantically dialed his number and smiled as it rang, and rang until the answering machine picked up. She slammed the receiver down on his mother's voice.

"No I don't want to leave a message!" she shouted and called again, and again.

"Mmph," Delilah hummed with a mouthful of dick. The phone ringing back to back to back was disturbing her rhythm. She paused the blow job enough to ask, "You don't need to get that?"

"I guess..." he said since it could be important since it rang back to back, to back. He watched her slide him back into her mouth as he picked up the receiver. "Hello?"

"Oh my God! It's you!" Jennifer moaned as if it had been years, not a week since they last spoke.

"Jennifer!" he reeled and stood straight up when he heard her voice.

"Owww!" Delilah groaned from having the dick roughly snatched from her mouth.

"I love..." Jennifer began until the female voice registered. "Is that a female? Ju got some bitch at jour house?"

"Uh, didn't you just get married? Your mother said you got married!" he shot back hotly. He couldn't believe she was complaining about him having female company when she had a whole husband.

"Yes but..." she pleaded and began to explain but it's hard to explain anything to anyone with a broken heart.

"Yes but nothing! That's fucked up yo!" he moaned but caught himself. His chest puffed with pride and he chumped her off. "You moved on and so have I!"

Buddha tried to hang the phone up but missed the cradle. He was in such a hurry to get back to Delilah he shrugged it off and pulled her onto the bed.

"Is everything ok?" Delilah asked as he fondled her pussy.

"I will be as soon as I get inside you!" he replied as he rolled the rubber onto his erection. "Can't believe this bitch tried to play me!"

"Bitch?" Jennifer reeled as if the word was a back hand slap. It was certainly the first time the spoiled girl had ever heard anyone call her one. Injury was soon added to her injury as she listened to Buddha fuck the white girl really, really good. Delilah squealed and squealed to orgasm after orgasm until Buddha grunted the grunt she knew so well as he filled up his condom.

She finally hung up the phone with a broken heart. It combined with that fierce Camacho pride and she was done with Buddha. It was just like that wise man said, love and hate in moderation because they could switch in an instant.

※

"Hey," Giggles greeted almost guiltily when he walked into the honeymoon suite the next morning. He was surprised to see Jennifer awake since she usually pretended to be asleep when he was in the room. Plus he fucked Rosalinda so good he actually did feel a little guilty. It was a guilty pleasure he would live with.

"Hey," she replied with a sly smile. She looked him up and down as if she just noticed how fine the man was. She been knew, it just never pertained to her, until now. Until after she heard the love of her life sexing the next chick a couple times until she couldn't take it anymore and hung up. Especially the mean things he said in between their sexual sessions. Broken hearted Buddha referred to her as bitch a few times as he lamented to the white girl.

"Hey?" Giggles asked, wondering why she was finally speaking to him. She pulled the comforter away to explain. He tilted his head curiously as he took in her curves. Rosalinda was on the chubby side of life, which was just fine but Jennifer was just perfect. In fact she was the most perfect woman he had ever seen. "Wow!"

"I want to wow too?" she giggled and the compliment and looked at his crotch.

"For real?" he asked. He nearly regretted the one for the road fuck he gave Rosalinda before they left their room not long ago.

His dick had no regrets and jumped at the prospect of fucking the fine young thing laid out in front of him. He had an impressive semi erection when he pulled his clothes off. The few years he had on Buddha made a visible difference. The difference between a young man and a grown man was obvious.

"Bente aqi," she summoned and waved him over with a finger. Her box bubbled and throbbed in excitement as she neared. She shocked them both when she pulled him straight into her mouth. She had never tasted pussy before so it's lucky her friend kept a fresh, clean one.

She sucked Giggle's dick so hard his knees buckled from the pressure. It was good it didn't dawn on him, it was too good for someone who was supposed to be so sheltered. His knees buckled again just like Buddha's used to do right before he bust a nut. Not that she minded but she needed him to come in her to get the get back she decided upon. She would give the next man Buddha's child and he would never know.

"I want you to fuck me," she announced. The words were barely out of her mouth before he was between her legs. Some dudes end up being the benefactor of the best sex in the world from some chick who's mad at the next man. Giggles was about to be that dude.

"Fuck!" he exclaimed just from the feel of rubbing the tip of his dick in the froth between her labia. It was hot and slippery so he slipped right in. Her box was still right and tight so he had to squeeze himself inside. They shared the first kiss of their life as he began to slow grind inside of her. She matched his rhythm like a sexual seesaw.

"Mmmm," Jennifer moaned when she realized he felt just as good as Buddha did inside of her. Better even, since she said fuck him for fucking the white girl. An orgasm crept up her legs and gave her soul a tingle. Giggles moaned and groaned as well since he felt the same sensation.

"Fuck!" he shouted as they both writhed from the mutual climax. He was surprised he had anything left after sexing Rosalinda all night, but felt spasm after spasm as he let loose the juice.

"Give it to me papi," Jennifer cooed, squeezed and rubbed his back as pumped her full of semen. A month later she could tell him she was pregnant, then give birth a month early. Her spoiled ego justified the ruse and she didn't care who cared. Only her mother would know and Esmeralda harbored far more secrets than this.

She did actually like not having to sneak around anymore. She and Giggles were married after all so she could flaunt him publicly. She did and they were a young, happily married couple by the time they made it back to New York.

CHAPTER 22

"So, fuck me huh? That's what niggas is saying, fuck Kev," Kev lamented when his count only counted up to a fourth of what it used to count up to.

"Buddha crew," Zero whined since he was feeling the pinch in his pocket as well. He was really hot since Buddha refused to put them down. Not yet anyway since there was touchy politics involved. Taking Kev's workers was a declaration of war, a war Buddha couldn't win yet.

"They caps bigger yo," Lil Bam offered in Buddha's defense. Crack heads are some of the most discriminating shoppers on the planet and loved a good deal. They could buy dimes from the Buddha crew and fill Kev's empty vials which left plenty to smoke for free. Ironically they were doing the same thing Joey was doing by repackaging the product. Except they had a right to since they bought it. Joey was just slimy.

"Yo, them niggas..." Kev growled and thought about the rest of that sentence. Those were some weighty words on the tip of his tongue so he mulled them over on his tongue before putting them out into the universe. Words are a lot like bullets in that regard. Once they fly they fly, and just as deadly. His two sidekick/workers hung on his every word and waited for the rest to come out.

"Nigga jumped my sister. Dissed my people..." Kev said as he hyped himself up. It was really about the money but that's plenty. "Yo, that nigga Buddha, he gotta go?"

"Go where?" Bam asked and strained his face to understand what he was saying. Both the youngins were shooters and shot plenty in defense of their projects. This was different, this was a hit. There's a difference between a shooter and a killer.

"You want us to murk that nigga B?" Zero asked and lifted his chin.

"I'm saying yo. Nawmean. We ain't even eating like we used to eat! And my bitches..." Kev moaned but stopped short of admitting he was tricking with a lot of the money they made him. As if the gold on his neck, fingers, ears and wrist weren't proof enough. Meanwhile they had new sneakers, weed to smoke and snacks to eat.

"What tho?" Bam urgently needed to know.

"He want us to off that nigga!" Zero cheered like he was up for the challenge. He definitely would get props for killing the legend in the making. The hood would know even if the cops didn't. The fame wouldn't last long because one of the Buddha crew would return the favor and kill him back, the first chance they got.

"Nawmean..." Kev replied. Bam twisted his lips dubiously at his dubious leader. Son couldn't pull the trigger on giving the order to pull the trigger but wanted them to go pull the trigger on the man. "Once shit get back to normal I'ma give y'all niggas a raise! Sixteen bucks off the 'huned!"

"Word," Zero nodded while his partner's lips twisted to the other side. A dollar could buy a bag of chips, quarter water, White Owl and a couple loose Newports but not a body.

"Word," Bam repeated because what choice was there. He sighed and went back to selling to the trickle of customers they had left. Once the Buddha crew shut down for the night it would pick up substantially.

※

"Son!" Rip grimaced as he walked into the apartment to sounds of sex. It was his fault for forgetting his gun and having to come back after telling Alva he was out for the night. He planned to do exactly what someone was doing to his mother. Rather vigorously from the sounds of it.

"Get this pussy! Don't play in it!" Alva demanded and threw it back. Rip tried to hurry and get out of there because no one wants to hear their mother getting dug out. Especially that good. "I'm about to cum all over that fat dick!"

"Please wait..." Rip laughed but she couldn't.

"Monte! I'm coming baby!" she screamed and froze her son in place. Sure, there are plenty of Montes in the word but chances are they didn't have his friend's voice too.

"I'm coming, too!" Monte shouted in his unmistakable, nasal voice.

"Huh?" Rip said, frozen in place. The weight of the gun in his hand became evident as he recalled the clear instructions not to touch his mother. His head nodded because his word was his bond. He said he would kill a nigga about his moms. Any nigga, including his own nigga.

"That's how you got me in this position now!" Alva

moaned over her shoulder and gave him a squeeze with her vaginal muscles.

"Doggy style?" he asked since that was the literal position they were in at the moment.

"Uh, pregnant papi," she snickered. His dick deflated instantly and fell out of her soaked snatch.

"But..." he began to whine until he looked down at his dick dripping with his and her juices. He may have been new to sex but smart enough to know how babies were made.

"Mmhm," she hummed and waited for his reply. He looked shook but shrugged and accepted his fate. "Come on baby father. Let me fix you a sandwich."

"I'll help," he offered and hopped up. They traipsed out in the nude since they were alone. Supposed to be anyway. The couple cackled happily until they reached the living room. They were halfway through before registering Rip sitting on the sofa.

"Gabby! What are you doing here!" she shrieked and covered her breast and box.

"I live here! The fuck is you doing here B?" Rip shot back. Monte's swinging dick answered that question so he popped up and aimed the pistol.

"Nooooo!" Alva screamed and jumped in front of her man. Rip tried to get around her to get a shot but she wouldn't allow it.

"Come on nigga!" Rip growled and snatched him by his neck since there was nothing else to grab. He dragged him out of the apartment and into the stairwell. His mother screamed at his back as he drugged him up to the roof.

"Gabriel!" she shouted but got no reply. She turned to Buddha's apartment and banged on the door. "Garrick! Buddha!"

"Fuck!" Buddha fussed since he and Delilah were making out real hot and heavy. He had whipped up a good froth between her legs from fingering her pussy when he heard his name over the banging on his door. He begrudgingly pulled his hand from between her legs and stomped to open the door. He was already confused but got even more confused when he saw his friend's naked mother. "I'm good yo."

"He, and him, and he's going to kill him!" she shouted and pointed at the stairwell.

"Him who? What are you talking about Miss Alva?" he asked and held her shoulders to calm her.

"Gabby caught my Monte and me. He took him up. He has his gun..." she managed. That he understood and tore off down the hall.

Buddha hopped the ten flights of stairs until he popped out the door to the roof. The sea of pebbles crunched under his feet when he emerged. He looked right until he heard voices to his left and took off. There was one of his closest friends holding a gun to the temple of another of his closest friends.

"Yoooo! Chill B," Buddha pleaded. "We family B."

"I told err body stay away from my moms yo. Didn't I?" he asked Buddha who had to agree.

"Yeah man but don't shoot him son. He's family," he reiterated while Monte stuck his chin up like he wasn't scared to die.

"I love her and she loves me!" Monte declared and lifted his chin a little more. The words seemed to affect Rip who began to lower the weapon.

"Don't shoot him yo," Buddha said softly and the gun came down some more.

"Nah, I ain't going to shoot him," he told Buddha and turned to Monte. "I ain't gonna shoot you B."

"Thank you," Monte sighed. He was ready to die but happy to live. They all started walking towards the stairs to go back down. The cat was already out of the bag so Monte figured it was a good time to share the news. "She's pregnant, with my baby."

"Who!" both Rip and Buddha turned and shouted.

"Alva. She's having my baby," he advised proudly. Buddha just shook his head and expected the gun to come back out. It didn't though as Rip walked back to where he was. He moved faster with every step until he reached a full sprint. He scooped him off his feet and dumped him right over the ledge of the roof.

"Noooooo!" Buddha screamed but it was too late....

The End

Stay tuned for We Run New York, part 2. In the meantime check out an excerpt of Young Pimping...

YUNG PIMPIN

Written by

Sa'id Salaam

CHAPTER 1

An evil smirk twisted Yung Pimpins otherwise handsome face as he spotted his target. The notorious Sammy the pimp was posted up at the bar talking loud and dressed even louder; old school to death in a yellow three-piece suit complete with yellow gators and yellow hat, with the long yellow feather extending from it. He couldn't help but wonder for a second if it was actually some place in nature where yellow alligators or ostriches thrived; perhaps some gay ass enchanted swamp with bull frogs giving each other blow jobs. But now wasn't the time to ponder over it, now was the time to kill.

Yung Pimpin represented the new era in pimpin. Instead of finger waves like his target, he wore an intricate array of braids running down to his shoulders. A crispy white wife beater showed off his lean muscular frame decorated with colorful tats. A diamond-laden 'YP' medallion hung to the middle of his chest on a diamond-crusted platinum chain. Expensive designer jeans low slung on his waist sat on top of exclusive sneakers.

The patrons of the speedy after hours' club grew quiet at the arrival of the highly-anticipated showdown. Rumors of the battle had the P&H bar filled to capacity. The joint was named after proprietors Paul and Harold 20 years ago but those who know, knew P&H now stood for pimps and hoes. This was Ground Zero, Pimp Central, Hoe Headquarters.

The sudden change in the air put Sammy the pimp on high alert. It was that eerie calm before the storm. The look in the soulless eyes of his bottom bitch confirmed the danger. There is no honor among thieves so the honorable thing would be for Yung Pimpin to bash the back of his head in then go shoot a game of pool until the cops came. No sense running because, again, there's no honor among thieves and someone was going to snitch on him.

"Heard you was looking for me." Yung demanded, tapping the man on the shoulder, making two mistakes at once. The first was talking instead of swinging and the second was touching instead of swinging. He paid for them both at the same time.

"I am!" Sammy said as he whirled around and swung. The open hand slap sounded like a thunder clap when it connected. A slap stings enough on its own but the razor blade concealed in his fingers made it burn. The slap was designed to humiliate but the blade served a more sinister purpose.

"Pimp fight!" a broke down old hoe named Debbie announced with glee. Her raspy voice had a slight echo from years of cum shots knocking out her tonsils. Her black lips where shaped in a perfect 'O' from all the dicks sucked. They looked like an old tire on her worn face.

The only thing better than a whore fight was a pimp fight and this bar had seen its share of both. Pimps when they do fight, fight to the death. Be the death literal or figurative, somebody had to die. Even if the loser lives, there will be no more pimpin for him around here. Lose a pimp fight and your stable and respect gets transferred to the winner. To the victor goes the spoils and in this case the booty is actual bootie. Pardon the oxymoron but no self-respecting hoe will whore for a pimp who gets punked.

"Get him daddy." Sammy's bottom bitch hissed like the snake she was.

Coming from her, it was another slap in the face and made Yung Pimpin hesitate. That hesitation cost him another slap in the face by the older pimp. This one was a Venus Williams backhand formally known as the pimp slap. It was the ultimate in disrespect. Even pimps don't like to be pimp slapped.

"Miss that good Wet-Wet don't you boy?" Sammy teased.

"You can take that bitch to hell with you." Yung snarled. He knew if he won she would be his again. This time he would do what he should have done many times over; kill her.

Yung lifted his hand to his face and felt the blood. The hand then turned into a fist and threw a straight jab that popped the pimp in his slick talking mouth. It was quickly reciprocated by a two-piece.

Both men shared the same height and weight among other things. The DJ cut the music and hit the lights so no one would miss the action. Camera phones began filming; this was going to be on world star.

"They kind of favor each other?" a young whore said with a curious frown.

"They should, they father and son." Wet-Wet reported.

She should know, she was part of the problem. It really wasn't about her but then again it was.

The pugnacious patriarch and progeny pimps went back and forth trading blows. The fight was pretty evenly matched with both lumped up and bloody when the inevitable happened.

Just like male Rams run full speed into each other with their horns and giraffes use their long necks to fight, pimps use straight razors. Once they got tired of punching, out came the blades.

"You know how to use that?" Sammy taunted and took a swipe.

The blow opened the front of Yung Pimpin's shirt and into his skin. The pain reminded him of the pistol in his pocket. He answered the question when he swung back, opening a similar hole in his father's yellow jacket.

Back and forth, blow for bloody blow, the father and son battled. It wasn't a battle of good versus evil, more like evil against more evil. You'll have to hear the whole story to determine which one was which.

Getting nowhere with the razors suddenly both Parker pimps pulled pistols. Only one got off a shot. One died, the other killed, again.

CHAPTER 2

Fourteen-year old Yancey glanced around the small section of the trailer that was designated the living room. The narrow aluminum box they called home was sectioned off into three bedrooms, a bathroom and kitchen. The flimsy material snitched on every move made within it. It creaked when you stepped or moved.

The muted squeaks coming from down the hall meant the guest chose heads over tails. There was no coin toss but there was a difference in price. So Yancey paid attention to it. Two more customers waited patiently for their own trip down the hall. What awaited there was relief. Just like a chiropractor can release soreness and stress by cracking backs, the woman behind door number one could suck your problems away; if only for a moment.

It mattered not that most of the patrons were married. Most live in the same run down trailer with wives and children. Only most wives wouldn't do what the woman behind door number one would do. That's why men paid Yancey to spend a few minutes down the hall. It was just like normal people pay to be entertained. Buy a book; rent a movie, Damita was Six Flags sexually. The Burger King of the bedroom, where you could have it your way.

"Whew wee that bitch got some fiyah ass head!" Roscoe exclaimed as he burst from the bedroom. He made the proclamation with the enthusiasm of one striking gold or oil. "Oops, my bad." He corrected, seeing a change on Yancey's face.

Barely in his teens, the boy was over six feet tall and had a natural muscle bound build men twice his age worked hard for. His one act of violence was sufficient for him not to be disrespected. Oddly, he didn't mind whatever Damita allowed men to do with her but didn't stand for her being disrespected either.

"My turn!" Fred cheered as if he made it to the front of the line in an amusement park; which in a way was accurate.

Fred only lived a few doors away with his three-hundred pound wife. She certainly couldn't get her legs up on his scrawny shoulders like Damita could. The wife was powerless to stop it so she pretended not to know.

Fred forked over a twenty which meant he wanted tails. The crumpled bill was hot and moist from being clutched tightly as he eagerly waited his turn. He rushed his tall frame down the hall and disappeared behind the door. The bed started creaking a few seconds later.

Yancey glanced up in frustration at the crooked ceiling fan. It too creaked and squeaked as it slowly rotated. The dusty device provided no relief from the brutal middle Georgia heat. Its only purpose was to circulate the menthol smoke of the customers. Still, it wasn't the fan that had young Yancey in his feelings.

He knew pimping a woman twice his age was wrong on

so many levels. The fourteen-year old had only had sex once before and was hooked. The memory alone gave him wet dreams every night that left him frustrated and embarrassed. He was a farm boy and realized that pussy was a cash crop. The steady flow of customers provided plenty of money when before there was none. Yes, it was wrong but it felt better than an empty stomach.

The bed groaned and squealed, then suddenly stopped. The two men in the room both sat up knowingly. After the time it took to pull his pants up, Fred emerged with that 'I just bust a nut' smile on his face. He made it quickly up the hall and out the door. He had to be home for supper. His wife turned a blind eye to his romps with the whore but made up for it if he was late for dinner.

"Here you go." Pastor Paul said smugly as he handed Yancey a ten dollar bill.

The boy hated the man's holier than thou attitude. It just didn't fit with buying pussy. He knew that if you ran the prints on that money it came straight from some old lady's purse. The congregation just bought him the new caddie out front so why not buy him a piece of ass too. Actually the ten he was spending meant he didn't plan on going any further than her tonsils. He only had sex with his wife; he was a pastor after all.

A few minutes later, he slinked out looking like he was ready for a nap. A good nut will do that for you. A strong orgasm is nature's number one sedative for both men and women. That's why you'll never hear this author's wife complaining she can't sleep.

Damita was right behind him. As he stepped out the door, she stepped to her pimp. She looked worn, well past the three score she had been on the planet. That's because crack heads live on a faster clock. Their days are five to one compared to normal people. It's like dog years in reverse. The sheer night gown she wore daily offered a view of what was left of her depleted figure. Yancey quickly snapped his head away not to see it.

"Half please." She demanded sweetly with her palm extended.

Yancey pulled out, counted, then split the day's receipts. She snatched hers eager to get to the dope boy, while his was going to keep bills paid and the fridge filled. She leaned down to kiss his cheek causing him to wince from her breath tart from semen, crack and Newports. Still he didn't pull away, no that would have been disrespectful.

"Want me to fix you something to eat 'fo I go?" Damita offered sounding sincere as if she meant it. It wasn't a lie; she just knew he would decline. She knew it was her duty to at least offer.

"No momma, I'm fine." Yancey told his mother's back, as she rushed to get dressed to go smoking.

The road that led to Damita Jackson being pimped by her own son was a bumpy one filled with pot holes, wrong turns and bad decisions. It started off innocently enough then went oh so wrong....

CHECK OUT SA'ID SALAAM ON AMAZON